HIS WORDS OF LOVE COULD NOT DROWN OUT THE WHISPERS

Laura returned from her honeymoon with the Earl of Dartmouth radiantly happy. Her new husband had awakened her to the true meaning of womanhood, and left her enraptured by his charm and his touch.

Never would she believe the rumors that he had savagely driven his first wife to her grave. *Never* would she imagine that he was driven by demons more powerful than any love. *Never* would she heed the warnings of a lord who once had wooed her that her life was in danger.

Then came her first taste of terror—and "never" turned to maybe. . . .

A
DOUBLE DECEPTION

A DOUBLE DECEPTION

by
Joan Wolf

A SIGNET BOOK

SIGNET
Published by the Penguin Group
Penguin Books USA Inc., 375 Hudson Street,
New York, New York 10014, U.S.A.
Penguin Books Ltd, 27 Wrights Lane,
London W8 5TZ, England
Penguin Books Australia Ltd, Ringwood,
Victoria, Australia
Penguin Books Canada Ltd, 10 Alcorn Avenue,
Toronto, Ontario, Canada M4V 3B2
Penguin Books (N.Z.) Ltd, 182–190 Wairau Road,
Auckland 10, New Zealand

Penguin Books Ltd, Registered Offices:
Harmondsworth, Middlesex, England

Published by Signet, an imprint of New American Library,
a division of Penguin Books USA Inc.

First Printing, October, 1983
14 13 12 11 10 9 8 7 6

 REGISTERED TRADEMARK—MARCA REGISTRADA

Printed in the United States of America

BOOKS ARE AVAILABLE AT QUANTITY DISCOUNTS WHEN USED TO PROMOTE PRODUCTS OR
SERVICES. FOR INFORMATION PLEASE WRITE TO PREMIUM MARKETING DIVISION, PENGUIN
BOOKS USA INC., 375 HUDSON STREET, NEW YORK, NEW YORK 10014.

I

Parents require in the man fortune and honour, which are requisite to make the married state comfortable and honourable. The young lady may require personal accomplishments and complaisance, which are requisite to render a union agreeable.

—*The Lady's Magazine*, 1774

1

In the autumn of 1814 Lady Maria Cheney
attended the wedding of her nephew, Commander the Hon. Mark Anthony Peter George
Cheney. It was an affair of much pomp and
circumstance, as befitted the alliance of two of
the oldest and most influential families in the
county. The history of the Cheneys stretched
far back into the days of the early Plantagenets,
and the present Earl of Dartmouth, Mark's
father, had been for forty years the most important man in Devon. The bride was Caroline
Gregory, and the Gregory family, while not so
illustrious or wealthy as the Cheneys, was quite
as old.

The marriage was celebrated in St. Peter's
Church, the parish church for Dartmouth Castle.
Surrounding the assembled congregation of
Cheneys were the memorials of their past: the
Dartmouth arms were on the pillars, Dartmouth
names adorned the windows, past earls were
buried behind the altar, and the churchyard

outside was filled with the graves of dead Cheneys.

The present heir to the earldom moved now from the sacristy to the front of the church to await his bride. Mark wore his naval uniform, and Lady Maria wiped away a surreptitious tear at the sight of his composed young face. She did not entirely approve of a boy of twenty assuming the responsibilities of marriage, but she was aware of the pressing need for him to do so. As the music began and the wedding procession started to moved down the aisle, she glanced at her brother next to her in the front bench.

The Earl of Dartmouth looked older than his sixty years. The death of his other son, Mark's older brother, Robert, had aged him badly. As she listened to the magnificent strains of the organ, Lady Maria reflected on that tragic event of just under a year ago. It had been such a freakish accident! Robert was a very good boxer. The blow to the head he had sustained had not seemed so serious at first. Concussion, the doctor had said. And then two days later he was dead.

She looked at Mark's clear-cut profile, and, sensing her regard, he glanced at her for a minute and winked. Then Caroline was at the front of the church and he moved to join her. The two young people ascended the altar steps, knelt, and the service began.

Robert's death had changed Mark's life more than anyone else's, thought Lady Maria as she automatically followed the prayers. As a second son, he had chosen the traditional Cheney profession of the navy. Not for Mark the land-owner's education of Eton and Oxford. He had gone to sea as a child and his schoolroom had been the cramped and turbulent cockpits and gun rooms of frigates. He had been a midshipman at eleven, a lieutenant at seventeen, and at nineteen he had been posted to the rank of commander.

Lady Maria was much afraid that Mark's naval days were ended. Which was a pity, because he had loved it so. Lady Maria treasured and still reread the letters he had written to her over the years. She was the closest female relative he had; his mother had died when he was seven.

Mark's job in future, she reflected, was to run the affairs of his family, his property, his county, and his country. His immediate job was to produce a son. Her brother had been quite clear on that score. The fragility of human life had been brought home to him most forcefully with the untimely death of the twenty-five-year-old Robert. Ever since Mark had arrived home six months ago, he had heard little else from his father but this one refrain: marry and get sons. The Dartmouth line, unbroken in six hundred years, must not be allowed to die.

Mark, however, had not needed much urging to marry Caroline Gregory. One look at her delicate beauty, her big blue eyes and shining golden curls, and he had been smitten. She looked entrancingly lovely today in her white dress and pearl-encrusted veil. You would have to travel very far, Lady Maria thought as the music started up again and the wedding party prepared to depart, to find a handsomer couple or one more probably destined for happiness. Everything about them matched: birth, fortune, beauty. And they were in love. Lady Maria sighed, wiped her eyes once again, and allowed her brother to take her by the arm.

The wedding breakfast was held at Cadbury House, the Gregory home on the outskirts of Dartmouth. It belonged now to Sir Giles Gregory, Caroline's older brother. He was twenty-six, the same age Robert would have been. The two of them had been at school together, Lady Maria remembered.

Lady Gregory, Caroline's mother, lived with her son, and she was the hostess for the reception. The church had been very crowded and a large number of the congregation arrived back at Cadbury House for some post-ceremony refreshment. As one would expect in Devon, there were a great number of naval men in attendance.

Lady Gregory, a dimmer, older version of Caroline, was a happy, not to say triumphant, mother of the bride. As well she might be, Lady Maria thought, her eyes on her nephew. That tall, slim young man with his splendid shoulders, his lithe carriage, his long-lashed golden-brown eyes—what mother would not rejoice to have him for her daughter? Not to mention the fact that he would be the Earl of Dartmouth one day.

Sir Giles was a courteous and conscientious host. He came in for a good deal of teasing from his own relations and from the Cheneys, most of which followed the lines of "your turn next." He took it in good-enough humor. Lady Maria thought there was occasionally a frosty look in his blue eyes, but to his credit, his smile never faltered. He had the reputation of being a very kind brother and a devoted son.

All in all, the day was a decided success. A highly desirable union had been forged, and all present had had a reasonably pleasant time.

Lady Maria accompanied her brother and assorted relatives back to Castle Dartmouth for the night. The family had given up living in the huge fortress of Dartmouth Castle almost a hundred years ago. The tenth earl, Mark's grandfather, had commissioned Nicholas Hawksmoor to build him a country house which would afford more comfort and convenience than the imposing fortification that had first been built in Norman times to guard the River Dart. The result had been Castle Dartmouth, so named to underline the fact that while it was a new location and house, the family had not changed. The house was generally held to be Hawksmoor's masterpiece.

The Earl of Dartmouth, his cousin Admiral Sir William Cheney, and his sister Lady Maria were the last to go to bed that evening. They sat together in the large, comfortable library, and the talk turned to Mark. The Admiral, evidently, had a point he was determined to make.

"I don't want to see that boy resign from the navy," said Sir William.

"Nonsense," replied the Earl gruffly. "He will have more than enough to occupy him here at home. I'm getting old. Can't do what I once did."

"You don't need to," put in Lady Maria. "You have a very well-trained and responsible estate agent. The estate practically runs itself anyway, and what else is necessary, Mr. Farnsworth is perfectly able to see to."

Her brother glared at her, and Sir William took advantage of his opening. "Maria is right. There is no reason why Mark can't keep his naval commission."

"Why should he?" grunted the Earl, staring at his cousin from under his formidable white eyebrows.

"Because Mark has shown exceptional talent as a scientific investigator. He is widely recognized by the Naval Lords as being the best hydrographer we've seen in years."

"Really?" said Lady Maria.

"Yes. The charts he's made of the River Plate in Argentina and of parts of the South Atlantic and Indian Ocean are the most accurate we have ever had. In fact, for the last few years he's been supplied with *three* chronometers—an extraordinary compliment, I assure you, that is usually accorded to only discoverers and navigators."

"He almost drowned in the River Plate," Lady Maria put in conversationally. "He was fourteen and had been sent out with the expedition to Buenos Aires. His ship was wrecked and quite a few men drowned—all for the want of an accurate chart. I think that's where his obsession for surveying began. But I did not realize his work was so well-thought-of."

"It is," said the Admiral.

"Well, this is all very interesting." The Earl rose to his feet. "Mark's duty just at present, however, is not to produce a chart, but a son. Good night, Maria. William." And he stumped out of the room.

2

In the spring of 1815 Lady Maria Cheney attended the wedding of her goddaughter, Miss Laura Dalwood. It was not as grand an affair as her nephew's wedding had been, but it was quite the most important thing that had happened to the Dalwood family in a very long time.

Lady Maria's childhood friend, Louisa Vincent, had married Sir Charles Dalwood thirty years ago. The owner of Dalwood Manor had at that time been a considerable man, if not in his county at any rate in his part of the county. The income from his estate had allowed him to live plenteously and hospitably, if not lavishly. However, as the years had gone by and the war had come and gone, the income from the Dalwood property became insufficient for the Dalwood family and house. With three sons to provide for, as well as a daughter, Sir Charles had been forced to cut back considerably on his standard of living, which was very unpleasant for everyone concerned.

Laura's marriage to Edward Templeton was the sort of solution to his problems that Sir Charles had occasionally dreamed of. Mr. Templeton had money—a great deal of money. He had moved to Devon eight years ago and had built Templeton Hall in the neighborhood of Sydenham Damerel. He had thus taken his place in the group of neighboring gentry whose homes were superior to that of Dalwood Manor. However, none of the surrounding houses—Templeton Hall in particular—had that thoroughly established look of old county position which belonged to Dalwood.

Sir Charles, poor though he may be, was still the most important man in his world. He belonged, belonged in a way that Edward Templeton never would. The Dalwoods had been true to their acres through the perils of civil wars, Reformation, Commonwealth, and Revolution, and the head Dalwood of his day had always owned and had always lived at Dalwood Manor. In his part of the county, the owner of Dalwood reigned supreme.

The marriage of Laura Dalwood to Edward Templeton was the marriage of ancient name and position to money; it was a type of alliance not at all uncommon in early-nineteenth-century England. However, as Lady Dalwood hastened to reassure her old friend Maria Cheney, she must not suppose that Laura was only marrying to please her family. "Edward is a charming man," she told Lady Maria. "Laura likes him very much indeed."

Lady Maria was exceedingly fond of her goddaughter. There was a serenity about Laura

15

that she found extraordinarily attractive. Laura had a gift for graceful stillness and repose that her godmother thought contrasted most pleasantly with the extreme shyness or noisy animation found most often in young girls her age. In fact, Lady Maria had quite made up her mind to offer to sponsor Laura for a Season in London when she turned eighteen. However, that would not be necessary now. Her parents appeared to have managed her affairs very well themselves. *If*, that is, the man was really acceptable.

It certainly did appear as if Laura was happy with her choice. Lady Maria arrived at Dalwood Manor the day before the wedding and was sitting in the drawing room having tea with Lady Dalwood when Laura came in to greet her godmother. She had just returned from a ride and her skin was still a little flushed with exercise. Her dark blue-gray eyes were warm with pleasure as she bent to kiss Lady Maria's cheek.

"Godmama! How good to see you. And how good of you to come for my great day tomorrow. You're looking very smart, as usual."

Lady Maria smiled affectionately at the smiling young face bent above her. In her old gray riding habit and well-worn boots, Laura most certainly did not look smart. But then, she did not have to, reflected Lady Maria wryly. Laura's hair was parted in the middle and drawn back smoothly against her head, a style becoming to very few women. Lady Maria looked for a minute at that smooth dark head and long graceful neck, and then she said softly, "Come and sit down and tell me all about your young man."

Laura complied. "Well, he is not precisely *young*, Godmama. Edward is thirty-three." Briefly Lady Maria's eyes met those of Lady Dalwood, and both ladies repressed a smile. After all, thirty-three does not seem young to seventeen, no matter how it might appear to two middle-aged ladies of fifty. "But he is very nice," Laura was going on. A gleam of laughter lighted her eyes. "And terribly handsome."

"Well, of course, that is most important," Lady Maria said imperturbably, and Laura laughed.

"It shouldn't be, I know," she replied. "But somehow . . . it is."

When Lady Maria saw Mr. Templeton at the church the following day, she realized that Laura had been speaking the simple truth about his looks. He was not a big man, but Laura herself was small, so that hardly mattered. And he was handsome—beautiful, almost, thought Lady Maria, regarding his fair-skinned, delicately chiseled face and his cap of shining golden hair.

The organ began to play, and along with the rest of the congregation, Lady Maria turned to look down the aisle to see the bride advancing on her father's arm. Sir Charles looked splendid and dignified next to the small white-gowned figure of his daughter. And Laura—she is so young, thought Lady Maria suddenly. All that gravity, that grace—and so young. She blinked away a tear. Good heavens, she scolded herself, I must be entering my dotage!

The entire Dalwood family had assembled beneath the roof of the Manor for Laura's wedding, and they were all in great spirits. As well they might be, Lady Maria reflected as she watched the oldest son, James, talking to his wife after dinner in the drawing room. She had had a very frank talk with Lady Dalwood the previous evening, and it appeared that Laura's marriage was nothing short of a godsend to the family. James, his wife, and their one child lived at Dalwood with his mother and father. Edmund, the second son, had taken orders and would take over the Dalwood living as soon as it became vacant—which would not be for another year or two at least. In the meanwhile, he was acting as curate for a neighboring parish. And Henry, the youngest son, had a commission in the Guards. All of the boys depended, in one way or another, on Dalwood for their finances. And Dalwood was mortgaged. Mortgaged to put three sons through Eton, two sons through Oxford, and to buy one son an army commission.

There had been nothing left for the daughter. But Edward Templeton had not wanted money with Laura, Lady Dalwood told Lady Maria. In fact, not to put too fine a point on it, he had paid heavily to get her. The mortgage on Dalwood had been redeemed and Mr. Templeton had given Sir Charles some excellent advice about investments. All in all, the financial future of the family seemed assured.

"He wanted a wife to give him consequence, I gather," said Lady Maria bluntly.

Lady Dalwood smiled a little. "Templeton

Hall is a much finer place than the Manor. But it wants that graceful beauty of age that Dalwood possesses. Mr. Templeton is a fine young man as well. And a gentleman. But he wants that security of position which only old families possess. Laura will give him that. She does like him, you know. We would never force her choice."

"Who is he, Louisa?"

"His father was in the City. Edward was sent to Eton and Cambridge, and when his father died he sold the business to a partner, came to Devon, and built Templeton Hall. I assure you, Maria, his manners are as gentlemanly as anyone we know. He himself never had any connection with the City. He is, like us, a landowner—only, unlike us, he is very wealthy. I have no fears for Laura."

Lady Maria wondered. It seemed to her that in their eagerness to acquire the Templeton money the Dalwoods had not inquired too carefully into the man's background. If he were interested in setting up as a rich landowner, why on earth had he chosen Sydenham Damerel—an obscure section of Devon that looked over the river Tamar into Cornwall? Lady Maria considered herself a great deal more worldly than her friend, who had spent the last thirty years buried in Sydenham Damerel. To Lady Dalwood, Sydenham Damerel was the center of the world. To Lady Maria it was rather an outpost of civilization. She was a little concerned about Laura, but at this point there was really nothing she could do.

3

Lady Maria had a house of her own in Bath, where she spent the greater part of the year, going up to London for a month or so every Season. When in London, she always stayed at Cheney House in Berkeley Square, which her brother the Earl was kind enough to staff for her visits. He himself rarely visited London anymore.

She was staying in Berkeley Square during May of 1815 when Mark also came up to town for a few days. Lady Maria had not seen him since his wedding; it was at Christmastime last year that Robert had died, and the Earl had had no heart for festivities this year. Consequently, she was delighted to hear from Robertson, the butler, that her nephew had arrived while she was out at a reception.

"Commander Cheney said you were not to wait up for him, my lady. He went to Watier's for the evening and said he would see you in the morning."

Lady Maria went to bed in a happy frame of mind, looking forward to a reunion with the boy she had always loved as well as if he had been her own son. She had been disappointed not to see him at Christmas and had tried to tell herself that his new duties and responsibilities made his coming up to Bath to see her an impossibility. Her brother was not well. And Caroline—happy, happy news—Caroline was expecting a baby. Mark was needed at home.

He was not at Cheney House when she arose in the morning, either. He had gone off to the Admiralty, Robertson informed her. It was not until almost noon that he returned, looking in on her as she sat in the morning parlor answering her mail.

"Good morning, Aunt," he said from the door, and came across the room to kiss her, tossing his hat on a sofa as he passed it.

"Mark!" Her strongly featured face was alight with pleasure. "How lovely to see you, my dear. And how splendid you look. William is right— you ought not to resign your commission. It would be a pity to give up that marvelous uniform."

He smiled a little. "As it happens, I am not resigning, Aunt Maria. I am on leave at the moment."

She took his hand and drew him over to a pair of chairs positioned near a sunny window. "Sit down and tell me about yourself. How is Caroline? My congratulations. I hear you are to be a father."

There was not a flicker of expression on his

face. "Yes," he said coolly. "Papa is beside himself with delight."

"And you?" she asked, disturbed by the look of him.

"Of course."

There was a brief pause, and then she said, "What were you doing at the Admiralty this morning?"

"I went up to see Lord Melville, the First Lord, and Mr. Dalrymple from the Hydrography Office. They wanted to know if I would undertake a survey of the coast of Ireland."

"And will you?"

The sun from the window gleamed on his thick light brown hair, flecking it with gold. He shook his head, and the lights in his hair danced. "No. What is needed first is a land survey of Ireland. And I cannot leave Castle Dartmouth at the moment. Papa is not well. I do not think he has long to live."

"Robert's death took the heart out of him."

"I know." Mark had always known that Robert was his father's favorite, just as he himself had been his aunt's golden boy. He smiled at her now. "It is good to see you, Aunt Maria. You at least never change."

"I suppose that was meant as a compliment," she said with dry humor. But she was not feeling at all amused. She was, in fact, alarmed. Something was the matter with Mark. He was almost unnervingly composed. And his smile did not reach his eyes.

"It *was* a compliment," he said decisively. "I have a few days to spare in London. Do you want an escort for any of your parties?"

Her sharp brown eyes were soft with affection as they rested on his beloved face. The planes of his cheekbones looked harder than she remembered. He had almost completely lost his boyish look. "You don't want to spend your evenings with an old woman," she said.

"Not with an old woman. With my favorite woman." And this time the smile reached his eyes.

She was deeply touched. She was also, upon reflection, deeply apprehensive. If she were his favorite woman, where did that leave Caroline?

After a week Mark went back to Devon, and in mid-June Lady Maria returned to Bath. Two weeks after her arrival home, the news from Castle Dartmouth arrived: Caroline had borne a son.

They called him Robert, at the Earl's request, and he was baptized with great ceremony at St. Peter's Church, where his parents had been married almost exactly nine months earlier. Lady Maria had not seen her brother so happy since before the other Robert's death. He had presented Caroline with a magnificent set of matched pearls and she wore them around her slender neck on the day of the christening.

Lady Maria thought that Caroline looked as if childbirth had taken a great deal out of her. She was too thin, too delicate-looking. Her great blue eyes dominated her narrow, pointed little face. She had not been able to nurse the baby, the Earl informed his sister. She was under orders from the doctor to stay in bed and to rest.

Mark was pleasant, courteous, attentive to his father, his wife, his guests. He did not appear to be overly interested in his son. Lady Maria found something slightly disturbing about his extreme self-possession.

The Earl of Dartmouth died in August. It was an occasion of sorrow for his family, but it had not been unexpected. Everyone drew consolation from the fact that he had lived to see his grandson.

It was the death of Caroline Cheney in October, almost exactly one year after her marriage, that shocked the family and the county. Lady Maria posted down to Devon from Bath immediately. It was Mark who gave her the dreadful news. "She killed herself, Aunt Maria."

"What!"

"Yes." The impression of formidable reserve he had given her on their last meeting was stronger now than ever. His face was absolutely shuttered. "She cut her wrist. I found her lying on her bed. She had been dead for several hours."

"Dear God, Mark!"

"Yes," he said again. "Quite." They were sitting in the library of Castle Dartmouth, and now he got up from his chair and went over to look out the window. "I have told the magistrates that it was an accident, that she was opening a letter and the knife slipped. No one believes it, of course, but they didn't dare ask too many questions. She will be given Christian burial from St. Peter's. I'll need you to stand by me, Aunt."

Lady Maria stared for a moment at his back. His broad shoulders looked absolutely invulnerable. "Of course I will stand by you, my dear. I am so terribly sorry."

He turned back to her. "One can always count on you," he said quietly. "Thank you."

Meeting his steady, unreadable eyes, Lady Maria understood why the magistrates hadn't been able to ask him questions. His air of remoteness daunted even her.

They buried Caroline the following day. Her mother and her brother sat with Mark and his aunt in the front of the church, and the grief that never appeared on her husband's face was all too evident on theirs. Sir Giles, in particular, looked shattered. He and Mark scarcely spoke, except for a few minutes at the graveside. At that time Lady Maria caught something in Giles's blue eyes that frightened her. Good God, she thought involuntarily, surely he can't blame Mark for this tragedy!

She stayed at Castle Dartmouth for several months after Caroline's death, running the house and helping to look after the baby. During that time it was made perfectly clear to her by a few of the upper servants, whom she had known for years, that Mark and Caroline had not been happy together. Why that was, no one knew. Lady Maria disliked gossiping with the servants, but the issue at hand was hardly one she could ignore. And she simply could not talk to Mark. On the subject of Caroline he was unapproachable.

They had not been happy. Mark, apparently, had always been scrupulously polite to his wife. But he had been distant. "He stayed away from her, my lady," Mrs. Irons, the housekeeper, told her bluntly. "He kept up a show in front of others—especially his father. But once the old Earl died, it seemed as if he even ceased to make that effort."

"But what could have happened?" Lady Maria asked in great bewilderment. "He was so in love with her."

"I don't know, my lady. But I do know that talk is circulating that it was his coldness that drove her to her death, poor lass."

"Oh, no!" cried Lady Maria on a note of pain.

"I don't like to repeat gossip, my lady," said Mrs. Irons a trifle grimly, "but I thought you should know."

4

Lady Maria stayed at Castle Dartmouth until the following April. She stayed mainly because she felt her presence helped in a small way to diminish the gossip about Mark. She had been alarmed and horrified by the extent and the malignity of that gossip. Where it came from or how it had started, she did not know. But people blamed him for the death of his young wife. It was there in their eyes whenever he entered a drawing room, a local meeting, the church. She felt that her presence was a demonstration of good faith on the part of his family and as such was necessary. She was not necessary to either the house, which was run most efficiently by Mrs. Irons, or to Robin, who was in the very competent charge of his nurse. She was needed, she thought, by Mark.

It was in April that she received a second shocking communication containing tragic news. It came this time from Sydenham Damerel. She was sitting staring at her letter in obvious distress when Mark came into the morning parlor. "What has happened?" he asked instantly.

She looked up at him. "What is it that Claudius says to Gertrude, something about sorrows coming not in single spies but in battalions? I've just received a letter from my old friend Louisa Dalwood. Her daughter, Laura, who is also my goddaughter, was married last year shortly after you were. Her husband is dead of typhus. He was only thirty-four."

"I'm sorry," said Mark. He came and sat down across from her on a rose-colored sofa. "It does not appear to have been a lucky year for marriages." There was a note of audible bitterness in his voice.

"No," she replied quietly. "Not, at least, for you or for Laura."

There was a pause, and then he said, in quite a different voice, "I had a rather important letter myself, Aunt Maria. From the Admiralty."

"Yes?" She looked at him inquiringly.

"They have offered me command of the frigate *Glasgow*. They want me to undertake a survey of the southern coast of Turkey."

"Turkey?"

"Yes." His golden-brown eyes, fringed by lashes many shades darker than his hair, were more alive than she had seen them in months. "The Turkish coast should be able to provide us with valuable naval ports. England has a steadily growing commercial interest in the Levant. The lack of anything but inaccurate charts of the south Turkish coast—almost four hundred miles of it—is a reproach to British exploration. Lord Melville writes that this expedition is being launched to remedy a serious chasm in geography."

"And they want you to command it?"

"Yes. I will be posted to the rank of captain." He grinned at her. "God, Aunt Maria, this is like the answer to a prayer!"

"But, Mark, for how long will you be gone?"

"Several years, I expect."

"Several years! But what about your son? What about Robin?"

His face darkened. "He has his nurse. He is only a baby. He doesn't need me."

Lady Maria was silent. After a minute he went on, his voice a little strained. "I think it will be better for everyone—Robin included—if I go away for a while. It will give old wounds a chance to heal. When I come back, perhaps I will be able to be a better father. But right now, I can't. I just can't."

It was the first crack she had seen in his composure. He was very pale. "If you want," she said gently, "I will stay at Castle Dartmouth."

"No." His eyes were brilliant with feeling. "No. You have done enough, Aunt Maria. More than enough. You have your own home, your own life. I appreciate more than I can ever say what you have done for me this last year. But I won't take advantage of you any longer. If you feel you can make an occasional visit to check up on Robin's welfare, I would be very grateful. But you have neglected your own life for my sake for too long. You must return to Bath."

In the end, that was what she had done.

Mark sailed for Turkey, and life for Lady Maria resumed its accustomed round. The situation at Castle Dartmouth remained stable for almost a year. Then Robin's nurse sent notice to Lady Maria that she was leaving her position. Lady Maria posted down to Devon at once. Someone else would have to be found to look after Robin, who was now a sturdy toddler of almost two. And, as she had received a disturbing letter from her goddaughter, Laura Templeton, in the same post as the nurse's resignation, Lady Maria dashed off an invitation to Laura to come to stay with her at Castle Dartmouth for a visit.

Laura thought she had never seen anything as magnificent as Castle Dartmouth. It was rather as if one had stumbled upon an Italian Renaissance palace in the midst of a mellow English landscape. The great baroque dome of the central hall dominated the building, which stretched out in graceful elegance over an indecent amount of space. To the west of the house were avenues of cedars leading to the stables and the hothouses. To the east was a glorious deer park studded with fine old oaks and graceful ponds. A fountain, which looked as if it might have been designed by Bernini, was the focal point on the south front lawn.

Lady Maria gave her goddaughter a house tour. "My father and my brother bought most of the furniture, pictures, statuary, and china that you see," she told the wide-eyed Laura. "We have some very fine pieces, I understand."

"Yes," breathed Laura, awestruck by the magnificence in evidence everywhere. "I should rather think you must!"

Laura was also introduced to Mr. Robert Cheney, age twenty-two months, and she immediately fell in love. Robin was an extraordinarily beautiful child, with bright golden curls and huge, angelic blue eyes. "However can she bear to leave him?" she asked Lady Maria after his nurse had taken him back upstairs for his supper. The two ladies were having tea in the family drawing room.

"Mrs. Stebbins' brother has retired from the navy and needs her to keep house for him. She has been kind enough to say she will stay until I can find a replacement, however." Lady Maria stirred her tea. "And now, my dear Laura, tell me about yourself. Are you sorry you sold Templeton Hall after your husband died?"

"No. I could not live there, Godmama. I'm not sorry I sold it." She sighed. "But I can't live at home either, it seems."

"Why not?"

"Oh, Papa and Mama are forever after me to 'do something with myself.' They want me to go to Bath. They want me to go to London. They want me to get married again is what it all comes down to."

"And you don't want that?"

"No!"

Lady Maria looked with concern at the lovely, unchildlike face of her goddaughter. "You are only eighteen, my dear. You will marry again one day."

"I don't see why," said Laura calmly. "I have money—more than enough to support myself."

She looked up from her lap to Lady Maria's face. "You never married, Godmama."

"That is true."

"You have a good life. You are allowed to have your own house, to go your own way."

"Is that what you want, Laura? To set up your own establishment?"

"Yes, I do. But Papa and Mama won't hear of it. They would not have complained if I had stayed at Templeton Hall, but when I talk of buying another house, they act as if they are horrified."

"I see." Lady Maria ran her finger gently over the decoration on her teacup and looked reflectively into Laura's smoky blue eyes. "I was not eighteen when I left home, my dear. I was twenty-nine." Laura opened her mouth to say something, and Lady Maria continued serenely. "Nor was I beautiful. You, on the other hand, are both eighteen and beautiful. Of course your parents are concerned about your setting up on your own."

"I am not a child," said Laura firmly.

"No, I don't believe you are." Lady Maria smiled at her reassuringly. "I think I may have an idea that would suit you. Let me think about it for a little."

"Oh, Godmama, I should be so grateful!" Laura sighed wearily.

In the end, Lady Maria made her suggestion and Laura fell in with it eagerly. She was to live at Castle Dartmouth for a time and help look after Robin. "I don't mean to suggest this as a permanent arrangement, my dear," Lady

Maria had said. "I don't wish to turn you into a governess. But as a temporary solution to both our problems, it may well serve."

The temporary solution served so well that it stretched from months into years. And the more time that passed, the more impossible it appeared that Laura would return to Sydenham Damerel. After the first year her parents protested that it was time she came home. After the second year they seemed resigned to their daughter's continued absence. Laura simply would not leave Robin.

She and the little boy had formed an almost instant bond and it was a tie that grew stronger with every passing day. Robin's nurse had been a competent, conscientious woman, but she had not had a warm personality. The child was starved for affection, starved for a mother. And Laura desperately needed someone she could love. It was not long before she was fiercely devoted to her small charge. She felt, in fact, like his mother.

Lady Maria came periodically to visit Castle Dartmouth, and with her came the only news they ever had of Robin's father. The Turkish survey was going very well, Lady Maria reported. "Besides his marine surveying, Mark seems to have become a determined antiquarian," Lady Maria told Laura on one of her visits. "The last letter I received from him was full of lamentations about his lack of Greek and Latin. Evidently the Turkish coast is studded with the remains of famous ancient cities. When he is not out in a boat, Mark appears to be an obsessive prowler of ruins."

"I thought all boys studied Greek and Latin," Laura observed.

"Mark did not go to school like your brothers, Laura. He joined the navy at age eleven, and while there was a schoolmaster on board to instruct the midshipmen, Greek and Latin was not part of his curriculum. He did manage on his own to acquire a much more liberal education than was offered. I've sent him literally hundreds of books myself. He reads French and Spanish. But not the classical languages—a gap which he is apparently now beating his breast over."

Lady Maria shared some of her nephew's letters with Laura, who was unabashedly curious about the father of her darling. Some of the things she had heard about Lady Maria's nephew had been decidedly sinister—very different from the picture that her godmother always painted of her nephew.

He certainly appeared to be a good naval officer and scientist, whatever else might be true of his character. He inquired periodically about the welfare of his son, but to Laura's alert sensitivity, the inquiries were definitely perfunctory. Quite clearly he did not care about Robin, a situation which only made Laura love the little boy even more.

The only person who seemed to care about Robin besides herself and Lady Maria was his uncle, Sir Giles Gregory. He lived at Cadbury House, a few miles from Castle Dartmouth, and came over at least once a week to visit his nephew. He was very fond of Robin, who was his only family since his mother had died.

Sir Giles was a handsome, eligible, well-off young man, and clearly he liked Laura. The neighborhood kept expecting to hear an announcement concerning the two of them, but somehow nothing more than friendship ever developed out of their relationship. Laura herself didn't quite know why Giles kindled no sparks in her breast. His blond, blue-eyed good looks, so like his nephew's, were certainly very attractive. He had given her clear indication on more than one occasion that if she gave him any encouragement he would declare himself. But that encouragement had not been forthcoming, and soon they settled into an easy comradeship that suited them both. Certainly it suited Robin, who was always delighted to see Uncle Giles. He was the closest thing to a father Robin knew.

On the subject of Robin's real father, Giles was reticent. He was willing to concede Mark's scientific and technical brilliance. But he always gave Laura the impression that it was an effort for him to speak well of his brother-in-law. In fact, Laura rather got the feeling that Mark's early years at sea had painfully hardened his character. "One sees so much cruelty in the navy," Giles said to her once. "The floggings, the impressments, the battles. Mark went into the navy when he was eleven, you know. I am not myself in favor of sending such young boys to sea. It cannot be good for their characters to be exposed at so young an age to the brutality of life on a ship of war."

Laura was inclined to agree with Giles about the folly of sending children to sea so early.

From all she had heard about him, it seemed that the Earl of Dartmouth was a tough character who had little concern for the feelings of others. His marriage had not been a success, and the blame for that was generally laid at his door. There was a very pretty girl in Dartmouth, now respectably married, whom Giles had pointed out to her once grimly as "my poor sister's rival." Mark evidently had not been faithful to his marriage vows for very long.

It worried Laura. She did not like to think ill of Robin's father. And she was afraid of what would happen when he returned. She had come to regard Castle Dartmouth as her home. Certainly the servants all acted as if she were the mistress of the house. She had made a number of friends in the neighborhood. And— surpassing all else in importance—she had her boy. What would happen when the Earl returned? It was an uncertainty that she tried to think of as seldom as possible.

II

The intent of matrimony is not for man and wife to be always taken up with each other, but jointly to discharge the duties of civil society, to govern their families with prudence, and educate their children with discretion.

—*The Lady's Magazine*, 1774

5

The first week of November brought some unusually fine weather to Devon, and Laura and Robin took full advantage of it. Robin had been given a pony for his fifth birthday in June and the two of them went out riding for hours every morning. On Tuesday they returned to the stables at one o'clock and were met by news that sent Laura's heart plummeting into her stomach. "His lordship arrived about an hour ago, madam," John, the head groom, informed her gravely.

Laura felt herself go white. "His lordship," said in that tone of voice, could mean only one person. "Thank you, John," she said a little tremulously. Then, taking a steadying breath, she turned to the child by her side. "Did you hear that, Robin? Your father has come home."

They walked together up the avenue of cedars, and Robin was unusually quiet. Laura took his hand and he looked up at her out of troubled blue eyes. "Do you think he will like me, Laurie?"

"Of course he'll like you, darling. He always asks after you in his letters to Aunt Maria; you know that. You might feel a little . . . awkward with him at first, but that will be only because you don't know each other." She reached over with her other hand to ruffle his sunny locks. "Don't worry about it."

Laura went in by the front door, something she rarely did, and Monk, the butler, greeted her with unusual solemnity. "His lordship has arrived, madam. He asked that you join him when you came in. He is in the library."

There was no mention of Robin, and Laura turned to him with a smile. "You go upstairs, darling, and wash up. I'll bring your father up to see you in a little while."

He nodded vigorously, gave her a little smile, turned, and raced up the stairs. Laura smoothed her own hair down and walked through the great domed central hall toward the library wing. She would bring Robin's father up to meet him, she vowed, if she had to knock him unconscious to do it.

The library door was open and she said from the doorway, "You wished to see me, my lord? I am Laura Templeton."

He was standing by a window looking out at the sunlit fountain on the south lawn, but at her words he turned. "Yes, do come in Mrs. Templeton. I am pleased to be meeting you at last."

He was still in front of the window and the sun was in Laura's eyes, blurring her vision.

The first thing she noticed was what a deep and beautiful voice he had. "We did not know you were back in England, my lord," she said.

He came around the desk and gestured her to a chair by the fire. "I landed in Deptford ten days ago and have since been paying courtesy calls on the Lords of the Admiralty. I suppose I should have sent you notice that I was coming." He shrugged slightly. "I didn't think of it. I'm sorry."

As he moved out of the glare of the sun and she was able to see him clearly, she was conscious of sharp surprise. He was different from what she had expected. He was very tall, all lean bone and muscle. His skin was deeply tanned from the sun but she thought, from the color of his hair, that he was naturally fair-skinned. There was little resemblance between his totally masculine good looks and the little-boy beauty of Robin.

"There is no need to apologize," she said, and essayed a smile. "This is your house."

He did not smile back. "I understand from my aunt, Lady Maria Cheney, that you have been looking after my son these last three years. I am most grateful." There was a flicker of expression in his brown eyes. "I must admit I had not expected you to be so young, Mrs. Templeton."

"I am twenty-two, my lord," she said shortly. He looked very elegant in his well-cut coat of blue superfine and his pale yellow pantaloons. She was conscious suddenly that the skirt of her riding habit was flecked with mud. He had wanted to see her right away, she thought defiantly. He could scarcely complain if she looked young and untidy. "I am quite old enough to be Robin's mother and I assure you I have looked after him as if he were my own." Her face softened. "He is a delightful child, my lord. So bright. So loving." She leaned forward in her chair a little. "I told him you would come up to the nursery to see him. Will you?"

"Yes." He looked utterly remote as he waited for her to rise and precede him out of the room. Please let him be kind to Robin, she prayed silently as they went up the two flights of stairs to the nursery.

Robin had taken her advice and scrubbed his face until it shone. As she came into his sunny blue-and-white room with the tall silent figure of his father at her back, he looked instinctively at her for reassurance. She smiled a little and said, "Here is your father, darling. Won't you come and say hello?"

Slowly Robin crossed the room until he was standing before them. "Hello . . . Papa," he said in an uncertain little voice.

"Hello, Robin," the Earl of Dartmouth said gravely. He looked for a long silent minute, scrutinizingly, into the child's face. The big, candid blue eyes looked back, unafraid. Then the man smiled. "You've grown into quite a lad. The last time I saw you, you were still wearing nappies. But you're not a baby anymore, are you?"

"No, sir," said Robin, beaming proudly. "I have my own pony even."

"Do you?" said his father with interest. "You must show him to me."

Robin looked lit from within. "I will!"

The Earl stayed in the nursery for perhaps fifteen more minutes, looking at Robin's toys, examining his schoolwork. Then he turned to Laura. "You must not let me disturb your routine, Mrs. Templeton. I know you and Robin must have things to do. Perhaps you will join me for dinner this evening?"

Laura was feeling immensely grateful to him for his handling of Robin. She had heard of his earlier indifference to his son. She had sensed a reluctance on his part to come upstairs with her. She had been terribly afraid that Robin was going to be hurt. So now she gave him her extraordinarily sweet smile and said, "Thank you, my lord. I should like that."

She dressed for dinner with special care, choosing an evening dress of deep blue silk that brought out the blue in her eyes. Her hair she wore à la Madonna, parted in the center of her head and coiled at the nape of her long slender neck.

She had no idea what they could possibly find to talk about and was relieved and pleased to find that the conversation did not lag. He had heard some of the details of the infamous trial of Queen Caroline for adultery that had been monopolizing the whole public and social life of the country since August and they discussed that debacle during the first few courses. "Thank God I was out of the country while that show was going on," he said over the soup.

"It was dreadful. The entire country simply ground to a halt. All the lords had to attend unless they were ill, recently bereaved, too young or too old, Roman Catholic, or, as in your case, out of the country. The House of Lords was too small to accommodate everybody, so Sir John Soane had to build a couple of temporary galleries. And in the end they threw the case out. The idiotic trial might just as well not have taken place." She shook her head. "It was so degrading."

His face wore what she had already come to think of as its shuttered look. "Unimaginable, that. Airing all one's dirty linen in public. It doesn't bear thinking of."

"No," said Laura fervently. "It certainly doesn't."

A pause fell in the conversation as they continued to eat their meal. Laura put down her fork, picked up her wineglass, and regarded him reflectively over its rim. The chandelier shining on his hair struck sparks of gold where the sun had bleached it. "Did you enjoy your Turkish expedition?" she asked. "Godmama said you had become quite an antiquarian."

He smiled. "I certainly caught the fever, but I lack the necessary classical background. I copied every inscription I could find, but my lack of Greek and Latin made the task very frustrating. I just about managed to puzzle out the names of emperors and the city in whose ruins I was wandering. I want to put the whole journey down in book form after I get the charts done for the Hydrographic Office. There has been almost no report of what is to be found on the south coast of Turkey since before Byzantine times. What I have to say may not be brilliant, but it will be better than nothing."

"What you need is a classics scholar, like my brother Edmund, to help you."

He looked interested. "You have a brother who is a classics scholar?"

"Yes. And I know he'd love to work on a project like this."

He nodded thoughtfully. "I may try to conscript him. But first I must attend to the charts."

He did not start work on his charts immediately, however. The next few days he spent with Mr. Farnsworth, the estate agent. And he scrupulously put aside a part of each day for his son. On Friday, to Robin's infinite delight, his father took him along on a tour of the estate farms. Robin rode his pony and was full of small-boy importance when they returned. From what he said to Laura, she gathered that the Earl had used the occasion of the ride to renew acquaintance with a number of his tenants. He could not have picked a better companion, she thought as she listened to Robin rattle on. The little boy knew just about every living creature on the entire estate—animal as well as human.

His father made a similar comment to her at dinner that evening. "I felt as if I were escorting Devon's most well-known face this morning. Even the dogs seemed to know him. Is he famous or notorious?"

Laura chuckled. "A little of both, I suppose. He has such a friendly nature. And I must admit I've encouraged his playing with the tenants' children. It's important for a child to have companionship."

"Yes." He looked at her soberly for a moment. "You have done a good job with him, Mrs. Templeton." Faint color stained her cheeks, and he went on, "He also appeared to be a head taller than most of the other children his age. Is that true?"

"Yes. Robin is very tall for five." She smiled at him. "In that respect he must resemble his father."

His golden-brown eyes never wavered from her face, but she could sense his withdrawal. It happened, she thought, every time she smiled at him.

6

On Saturday Lady Maria arrived at Castle
Dartmouth. Mark had gone out with Mr. Farnsworth, so it was left to Laura to greet her.

"My dear, I was so surprised to receive Mark's
note yesterday. Whatever was he thinking of,
to come down here when he must have known
you were alone with Robin? It is not at all
proper for you to be in the house with him
without a chaperon."

"A chaperon!" said Laura in a startled voice.
"Surely I am past the age of needing a chaperon,
Godmama."

"Of course you are not past the age of needing a chaperon. You are twenty-two. And Mark
is twenty-six. Really, I am very annoyed at
him for his thoughtlessness."

Laura was conscious of deep surprise as
Mark's age was mentioned. That composed and
unrevealing face looked older than twenty-six.
It was a face that guarded its thoughts and
feelings well. She had spent rather a good deal

of time with him these last few days, but she knew him no better than she had after their first dinner together. He was always courteous and coolly charming, but he kept himself to himself.

"I think you are being silly, Godmama," said Laura now. "I am Robin's governess. Lord Dartmouth is his father. There is nothing at all odd or improper in our living in the same house."

"You may think I am being silly, my dear, but I assure you the world will think as I do. And you are not Robin's governess. You are my goddaughter. I was not aware that we paid you a salary for taking care of him."

"Of course you don't pay me to take care of Robin! I do it because I want to, because I love him."

"Precisely. In short, you are not a governess at all, but an attractive young woman of birth and fortune."

"I'm a widow!"

"A very young and lovely and rich widow," replied Lady Maria dryly. "That's even worse." Then, as Laura looked distressed, she continued soothingly, "Well, I am here now, so you needn't worry for the present."

The butler came into the room with the tea tray, bringing what was for Laura a welcome interruption. She had found Lady Maria's words very upsetting.

When the tea had been poured, Lady Maria sat back in her chair and regarded her goddaughter appraisingly. Laura was wearing a matching bodice and skirt of wine-colored merino. It was simple and smart, and Lady

Maria regarded it with approval. She approved also of the swept-back brown hair, smooth and dark as polished wood. She saw with satisfaction the worry in the dark, smoky blue eyes. She smiled gently and said, "How do you like Mark?"

"He seems very nice," replied Laura evasively. "Robin is thrilled with him."

"Ah," said Lady Maria. "They have become friends?"

"Yes," said Laura, and saw the flicker of relief that crossed her godmother's face. So it was true. Mark had not previously been interested in his son.

"I am glad to hear it," Lady Maria said smoothly. "They have not seen each other for such a long time."

"Four years," said Laura.

"Yes. Too long."

There was a step in the hall and then a tall presence filled the doorway. "Aunt Maria," said Mark's quiet voice.

Laura had never seen her godmother look so beautiful. She held out her hands to her nephew. "So, my dear, you have returned at last. How did you leave the Turks?"

He came across the room and gathered her for a moment into his arms. Then he stepped back and smiled down at her. "Unhappy," he answered. "The local aga at my last port of call offered me two hundred piasters for a young midshipman who had taken his fancy. He wasn't at all pleased when I refused."

She laughed as she was meant to. "You are a dreadful boy." Then, as she took in the

49

whipcordlike toughness of him, the stripped austerity of bone and muscle, her eyes narrowed. "No," she said slowly. "Not a boy any longer."

"No, Aunt." His teeth were very white in his bronzed face. "Not a boy. A ship's captain, if you please."

"Was the survey a success?"

"It was a success. The Admiralty Lords appeared to think so at any rate." He sat down and accepted a cup of tea from Laura. "I've been out with Farnsworth. We went over to Dartmouth Castle. The estate appears to be in good trim."

"Yes, Mr. Farnsworth is very able. But there are *some* things, Mark, that require your attention."

He sighed. "I know, Aunt Maria. An absentee landlord is highly undesirable. You will be happy to hear that I intend to remain at home for quite some while."

Laura heard his words with a sinking heart. She had not realized how deeply she was hoping that Robin's father would go away on another lengthy voyage. But he was going to stay here at Castle Dartmouth. Her throat was dry as she sipped her tea. Where was that going to leave her?

Lady Maria evidently had the same idea. "It was very thoughtless of you, Mark, to come down to Devon before I was here. We have Laura's reputation to think of. After all, we owe her a great debt of gratitude for all that she has done for Robin."

Laura began to protest, and Mark looked

distinctly startled. "Her reputation? What do you mean, Aunt Maria?"

"I mean that she is young and unmarried and ought not to be living unchaperoned in a house with an unattached man. You don't want to compromise her, do you, Mark?"

"Godmama, you are being ridiculous!" said Laura hotly, but Mark, after a minute's reflection, disagreed.

"No, she is simply being realistic." He looked charmingly rueful. "The thing is, Aunt Maria, I had no idea that Mrs. Templeton was so young. It never crossed my mind that I might be putting her in an awkward position."

"Well, let us hope that no permanent damage has been done. I am here now and we will all three attend church together tomorrow. Who is to know when I arrived?"

"The whole neighborhood," said Mark a trifle bleakly. "When was anyone ever able to keep a secret in this house?"

It seemed he was right, for no one appeared at all surprised to see him at church the following morning. After the service he stood in the cold November sunlight, flanked by Lady Maria and Laura, and the gentry of Dartmouth flocked to greet him. There was curiosity in many eyes, and reservation on many faces, but they all came and they all spoke cordial words of welcome. There were Mr. and Mrs. Charles, Sir Ralph and Lady Monksleigh, Lord and Lady Countisbury, the Daltons, and Sir Giles Gregory, to name the most notable.

Giles took Laura aside to say quietly, "I am

glad to see Lady Maria. I had heard that you were alone at Dartmouth Castle. That won't do, you know, my dear Laura. Not with Mark."

Laura felt her temper rising. "Why ever not?" she asked sweetly.

He looked at her out of worried blue eyes. "I don't mean to suggest anything sinister. It is only that Mark has a certain . . . reputation. Perhaps he has changed. God knows, I hope he has. He is a man of brilliant talent. It is such a shame to see his abilities soiled by the more . . . immature aspects of his character."

"Just what are you suggesting, Giles?" said Laura forthrightly.

He smiled a little tiredly. "I'm sorry. Don't pay any attention to me. I suppose I just can't forgive him for what happened to Caroline. Which is unfair of me, I know."

"Uncle Giles!" came a clear child's voice. "Did you know my papa was home?"

Robin was among them, and his presence did a good deal to break down the constraint that had been evident between the two men. He was so obviously proud of his father, so fond of his uncle, so carefree and full of life, that in a short while they almost appeared to be the family party that they were. Giles even accepted Lady Maria's invitation to dinner.

Another two weeks went by at Castle Dartmouth, and Mark began the work of recording his survey. Letters began to arrive for him in great numbers, letters from prominent antiquarians, travelers, and scholars. Lady Maria, looking at a letter from Major James Rennell, the foremost geographer of Britain, was rather awed. Evidently Mark's reputation as a man of science was far greater than she had ever realized. His survey of the coast of Turkey, as yet unrecorded and unpublished, had already taken its place in the scientific world.

His reputation as a scientist was assured. His personal reputation, while gaining ground, was not yet secure. The memory of his tragically dead wife still lingered in Dartmouth. Lady Maria thought there was only one way the ghost of Caroline would ever be put to rest, and she set about rectifying matters with her usual tactful care.

"Whatever are you going to do with Robin when Laura leaves?" she asked her nephew one afternoon as they drove back from a visit to an elderly pensioner of the family.

"Leave?" he said. "Why ever should she leave?"

"She cannot stay here with you alone, Mark. Surely I have already made that clear to you. And I must be returning to Bath shortly."

His brows were tense with irritation. "It's ridiculous. She loves Robin. She has no wish to leave him. His heart will be broken if she goes. And all because some old gossips may talk!"

"They *will* talk. Laura may say she won't regard them, but we must not take advantage of her affection for Robin. Nor would her parents permit her to remain."

"She is her own mistress, surely," he said shortly.

"Mark!"

There was silence as he turned a corner.

Then he said more quietly, "What do you suggest, Aunt?"

She sighed unhappily. "I don't know, my dear. You are right when you say losing Laura will break Robin's heart. If only there were some way she could honorably stay!"

The horses stopped and, startled, she turned to find herself the target of a disconcertingly shrewd brown gaze. She didn't say anything, and after a moment Mark drew a long quiet breath and then expelled it. "All right, Aunt, you have made your point."

"You will think about it?" she asked hopefully.

"I will think about it." He turned his gaze to the road and set the horses into motion once again.

He thought about that conversation on and off for two days and then he asked Laura if he might see her privately in the library. He had caught her as she and Robin were coming in from their morning ride; evidently he had been on the lookout for her. She agreed in a tense voice, sent Robin upstairs to change, and accompanied Mark to the room he had taken over as his own.

There were a number of papers on the desk, all arranged in neat piles. She caught a glimpse of a map that was clearly in the early drawing stages and then she moved to take the chair he had gestured her to. A feeling of *déjà vu* crossed her mind; just so had they sat on the day of his return. She even had on the same riding habit. She took her hat off and put it down on the table next to her, followed by her gloves. A long strand of hair had come loose from her chignon and she tucked it back again with unsteady fingers. Her heart was hammering. He was going to send her away; she knew it. She sat, mute in her distress, and looked at him out of slate blue eyes.

"I should like to discuss Robin's future with you, Mrs. Templeton," he began. She nodded, afraid to speak, and he went on. "My aunt will be leaving for Bath shortly, and she is adamant that you cannot stay here with me without a chaperon."

"Lord Dartmouth, please be assured that I do not regard a chaperon as at all necessary. I am a widow, twenty-two years of age, and I have been taking care of myself very adequately for four years. I should be happy to stay here with Robin indefinitely." She spoke with great earnestness, leaning forward a little in her anxiety to persuade him.

He was looking very serious. "You really love him, don't you?"

"Yes. I will do anything to stay with him."

The gravity of his expression gave way to a look of faint amusement. "Will you?" he murmured. He leaned back in his own high-backed chair and surveyed her coolly. "You cannot stay here unchaperoned. I have enough to live down with my neighbors without adding *that* to the tally." It was the first reference he had ever made to his precarious reputation. She could feel her throat beginning to ache and tears prickling behind her eyes. Desperately she tried to beat them back, and so only partly heard his next words.

"*What* did you say?" she asked incredulously.

"I said you could stay if you married me," he repeated calmly.

"M-married you, my lord?" she faltered.

"Yes, Mrs. Templeton. I am asking you to marry me. It seems the best solution all around."

"Solution?" she echoed, staring at him and trying to see if he were really serious. It was hard to read his face. His surprising lashes, long as a girl's in that thin, masculine face, were half-closed over his eyes. She wondered if that remote, guarded look of his hid a deep hurt or whether he truly was as unfeeling as he appeared. Either way, it was a disturbing expression for a young man of twenty-six to be wearing.

"Yes, solution," he repeated patiently. "From my point of view, our marriage would have several advantages, the chief of which will be to gain you as a mother for Robin."

"I see. And I would not have to leave him."

"Precisely."

"But . . . marriage! Surely there is some other way, my lord. We scarcely know each other."

"We know enough, I should think," he returned levelly. "Mainly I know that you love Robin and that he loves you. I do not want to have to separate him from you. And, then, I shall have to marry again anyway. One child is not sufficient to secure the succession."

She felt a cold shiver run down her spine. He sounded so callous. "From your point of view, the arrangement would have merit also, I believe," his cool voice was going on. "You are comfortable here at Castle Dartmouth. You have friends in the neighborhood. You will not find me an unreasonable husband. Come, Mrs. Templeton, let us be practical. You are not, as you pointed out earlier, a green girl. You have been married before."

"Yes," Laura said colorlessly. She looked at her hands lying clasped together in her lap. "May I have a little time to think about this, my lord?"

"Certainly." He rose to his feet, indicating the interview was over. "There is no hurry—so long as Aunt Maria remains."

"Yes," said Laura stiffly. "I understand that perfectly. I shan't keep you waiting for long." With proud grace she turned her back on him and left the room.

7

The first thing Laura did, before even changing out of her riding habit, was to seek out Lady Maria. That lady was sitting in the morning parlor working on a lovely piece of embroidery when Laura came breathlessly into the room. "Godmama, I must talk to you! The most extraordinary thing has happened. Lord Dartmouth has asked me to marry him."

"Has he?" Lady Maria put down her embroidery and turned a delighted face to Laura. "I must say I hoped he would do so. It is such a perfect solution."

"Solution," repeated Laura, and abruptly sat down. "That is how he described it also."

"Well, it is, my dear. Surely you must see that. It solves the problem of Robin, which is the main thing, of course. And you are just what Mark needs. You are respected and esteemed by all the neighborhood. Marriage to you will bury all those unpleasant rumors forever."

"I am glad it will be so beneficial to Robin and to Lord Dartmouth," Laura said tartly. "I suppose it is selfish of me to consider my own welfare in all this."

Lady Maria looked with concern at the flushed cheeks and snapping eyes of her goddaughter. "My dear, of course your welfare is of importance to me," she said soothingly. "Such a marriage has many benefits to you as well. If you marry Mark, you will have one of the best positions in the country. You will be the Countess of Dartmouth. Castle Dartmouth, the most beautiful house in England to my mind, will be your home. And where will you find a finer, more splendid young man than Mark? He is handsome, rich, wellborn." Yes, thought Laura to herself, and his first wife committed suicide after only a year of marriage. But Lady Maria appeared oblivious of the darker side of her nephew's character. "He is a brilliant young man, Laura, and a wife like you is just what he needs to enable him to regain the equilibrium he lost with that tragic event of five years ago."

They appeared to be back to Mark's needs again and Laura looked with resignation at her godmother's handsome, faintly lined face. With Lady Maria, she realized, Mark would always come first. This was a decision she would have to make for herself.

She went to her room after first checking on Robin and setting out some puzzles for him to work on. She took off her boots and her jacket and lay down on her bed and stared at the ceiling. She would think this over very rationally, she told herself. She had been offered a marriage of convenience and she must decide if it would indeed be convenient for her to accept.

There had been some truth in all that Mark and Lady Maria had said to her. She did like Castle Dartmouth, she did feel at home here. She would be sorry to leave. She looked around her familiar bedroom, with its pretty hangings, its comfortable chaise longue and well-appointed writing table. She had been happy here. She had been safe.

But if she married Mark, this would no longer be her bedroom. There was the rub. He was proposing a convenient marriage to her, not a nominal one. He had made that quite clear. He needed more sons—in case, she thought bitterly, Robin should die. She would have to move into the big bedroom that adjoined the Earl's room that Mark slept in. She had been in there occasionally before he had returned home. She thought suddenly of the big four-poster bed that stood so majestically in the middle of the room, and she shivered. She couldn't do it. He was a stranger and she had a suspicion that he would always keep his distance from her. But that would not stop him from doing his duty. No, she couldn't do it.

Someone knocked on her door and she called, "Yes?" A golden head peeked into the room.

"Laurie? I came to see if you were all right. You looked peculiar before. And I finished my puzzles."

She pushed herself up on her pillows. "I had a headache," she said, "but I'm better now."

He came into the room and climbed up next to her on the bed. "Would you like to read me a book?" he asked hopefully.

She looked into her boy's beautiful little face and forced a smile. "Go and get one," she said gently. Then, as he scrambled off the bed and headed for the door: "And, Robin, walk! I'll still be here when you get back."

She watched him slow down and close her door carefully behind him; then she lay back and once again regarded the ceiling. She didn't know what she had been making such a fuss about. She had no choice, really. She had to be here when he got back. She would tell Lord Dartmouth that she would marry him.

Mark had not seemed surprised by her answer. Nor had he seemed terribly pleased. She had made the sensible decision, he told her pleasantly. When would she like to set the date?

Laura didn't know, and Lady Maria was called in as a consultant. If the prospective bride and groom were noncommittal, she more than made up for their lack of enthusiasm. She kissed Mark. She kissed Laura. She called for champagne. She got out a calendar, and pen, and some paper and sat down to make plans.

Laura and Mark agreed with almost everything she suggested. First a notice had to be sent to the newspapers. Then the banns had to be called. "There is no point in delaying for too long," Lady Maria said briskly, and the two young people agreed woodenly.

"Now, where shall you be married from?" she asked finally. "Castle Dartmouth?"

"No!" said Mark violently. Both women stared at him in surprise. Beneath its bronze sunburn his face was very pale. "No," he said again, more quietly but with utter finality. He went over to the window and looked out.

Lady Maria stared for a minute at his back, and then she turned to Laura. "Well, then, we'll have the wedding at Sydenham Damerel."

For the first time since she had known him, Laura understood perfectly how Mark felt. "No," she said, and he turned to look at her.

"London," he said at last to his aunt. "We'll be married at St. George's, Hanover Square. Then Laura and I can stay at Cheney House for a few days. Perhaps you would be good enough to take Robin in charge for a week or so, Aunt Maria."

"Of course, my dear. It sounds an excellent scheme."

"Laura?" He looked at her, raising an eyebrow. She was no longer "Mrs. Templeton," she noticed.

"Yes. That sounds fine."

Lady Maria beamed. "Well, then, Mark, write out the announcement for the papers and send it off. And, Laura, you must write to tell your parents. They will want to come up to London for the wedding."

"Oh, I don't know," said Laura uncertainly, and Lady Maria slapped her calendar down on the desk.

"They must come. This wedding must go according to proper protocol. I don't want any detail neglected that might lead to scandal. Remember, Laura, you *were* alone here with

Mark for almost a week. We must think of your reputation, my dear."

"Laura's reputation is irreproachable, Aunt Maria, and you know it," said Mark coolly. His hands were in the pockets of his riding breeches and he was regarding his aunt with some austerity. "Don't try to intimidate her. It is *my* reputation you are concerned about." He turned to Laura. "You must do as you please about your parents."

Laura met his eyes for a minute and then she turned to Lady Maria. "They will come. You are right. There must be no gossip." She smiled slightly. "For Robin's sake."

Lady Maria looked relieved. "Excellent. I will make arrangements about where they can stay. And after the wedding breakfast I will bring Robin back to Devon and await you here. That will give the two of you a chance to have a little honeymoon by yourselves in London."

Laura barely repressed a shiver at her words.

Everything went off exactly as Lady Maria suggested. Sir Charles and Lady Dalwood came over to Castle Dartmouth for a few days to meet Mark, and Sir Charles and he came to an agreement about marriage settlements. Sir Charles was very pleased with his daughter. Her first marriage had been a profitable one; this marriage was absolutely brilliant. Edward Templeton had had money; the Earl of Dartmouth had more: he had property.

Two weeks before the fatal date, Laura went up to London with Lady Maria to shop for a trousseau. She had never in her life been to

London before and normally she would have been thrilled by her first sight of the famous city, but apprehension destroyed all her pleasure in her new clothes and new surroundings.

Mark and Robin arrived three days before the ceremony, and Laura enjoyed herself more than she had in weeks on their expeditions to see the beasts at the Tower and the marvels of Astley's Amphitheater. Mark was more natural and approachable than she had ever known him on those occasions, and the tension inside her relaxed a little.

On the morning of her wedding it was back in full force, however. Her maid dressed her in the pale rose sarcenet morning dress she and Lady Maria had chosen. She felt as if she were a sleepwalker moving through a dream as she got into the crested carriage that was to take her to Hanover Square.

Her somnambulist sensation continued throughout the ceremony and the wedding breakfast that followed. Then Robin got sick to his stomach. Too much excitement and too much food, his father diagnosed, and made him lie down, after which he fell asleep for two hours. When he woke up he was right as rain, and Lady Maria determined to make a start on their journey back to Devon. Laura protested, but her godmother was adamant. "There is a very good inn about twenty miles out of London we can easily make before it gets dark. You and Mark must be left to yourselves for a while." And she packed up Robin and took him away, leaving the newly married couple alone together at Cheney House.

"Put on your riding habit," Mark said to her as they returned into the house after waving Robin off. "We need to get some air."

Laura was delighted by any idea that would put off the moment when she would be alone with him, and complied with his suggestion with gratifying alacrity. The January day was cold and the park almost deserted and they had a pleasant hour cantering by themselves under the barren trees. Laura's magnolia skin was rosy with cold and exercise when he said, "It's getting dark. Time we started back home."

She was riding beside him in silence through the London streets when both their attentions were caught by a man's voice crying out, "Commander Cheney! Is that you?"

Mark pulled his horse up immediately and Laura followed suit. "Yes," Mark said. "Who is that, please?"

"It's Evans, sir." A man came out in the street to stand beside Mark's horse. "Gunner, from the *Brand*. Do you remember?"

"Of course I remember you, Evans," Mark said quietly, looking at the upturned face. "How are you these days?"

The man at his side was thin and haggard and desperate-looking. "Not well, sir. That's my wife and child over there." He nodded to a woman huddled on the curb holding a baby. "We've just been evicted from our rooms. I've no money, sir. Nowhere to go."

Mark was dismounting before he had finished speaking. "How long have you been out of work?" he asked tersely.

"Four months, sir. I haven't been able to get

anything steady. Not since I was paid off two years ago."

Mark was signaling to a hackney. "You can come home with me for the night, Evans," he said, opening the door. "We'll see what we can do for you in the morning." He took the thin arm of Mrs. Evans in his hand and helped her into the cab. "Cheney House, Berkeley Square," he said to the driver, and closed the door on the couple's incoherent thank-yous.

He mounted his horse again and walked him over to where Laura was waiting for him. "I'm afraid I've just saddled you with some uninvited guests," he said quietly. "I'm sorry, but it couldn't be helped."

"There is nothing to be sorry about," she returned. "Those poor people! Whatever would have happened to them if you hadn't come along?"

He looked very bleak. "It is nothing unusual, Laura. It happens all the time. There are simply no jobs for all the demobilized soldiers and sailors who have been thrown on the economy since the war. Too many men who fought for their country are ending up like Evans: homeless, jobless, destitute. In some ways the peace is worse than the war."

They were trotting briskly through the quickly darkening streets and arrived at Cheney House almost simultaneously with the hackney. Laura took one look at the thin, pale, frightened face of Mrs. Evans and put an arm around her comfortingly. With calm efficiency she issued orders to the servants, and in an hour's time Mr. and Mrs. Evans and baby were fed and tucked up in a warm room with a roaring fire and a big comfortable bed. Then Laura and Mark changed clothes and had their own dinner. It was ten o'clock by the time they finished and Laura rose to leave him to his wine. "I'll await you in the drawing room," she said as she stood facing him over the candlelit table.

He had stood up when she did, and now he smiled and shook his head. "No," he said. "I don't want any more wine." He started coming around the table toward her. "Poor Laura," he said. "What a wedding day! First a sick child and then an indigent family to feed and put to bed."

"It has certainly been unusual," she said a little breathlessly.

He was very close to her now and there was a smile in his eyes. "It's time we put ourselves to bed, I think."

In the light of the candelabrum he looked very handsome, and as she looked up at him, very big. "Yes," she said. "Yes, I suppose we should." And she walked beside him up the stairs to their bedrooms.

8

Laura's maid was brushing out her hair when the connecting door between their bedrooms opened and Mark came in wearing a silk dressing gown. After a quick glance at him, Laura remained perfectly still, looking at her reflection in the mirror. She wore a lacy white negligee that was cut low enough to show off the creamy silkiness of her shoulders. "Shall I plait it, my lady?" the maid asked.

"No," said Mark. "Leave it as it is."

The maid put the brush down, leaving Laura's hair falling dark and shining down her back. "Will that be all, my lady?"

"Yes," said Laura. "That will be all, Potter."

As the door closed behind the maid, Mark came across the room. She did not hear his feet on the thick carpeting and started a little when he appeared behind her in the mirror. She was sitting on a quilted silk stool and he rested his hands on the nape of her neck, his fingers against her hair. "I have often wondered what it would look like down," he said softly. "It is beautiful."

She sat perfectly still, as if frozen into immobility. "Laura?" he said. She tipped her head back a little to look at him and he bent forward and kissed her throat. He was still standing behind her and his hands pulled her back against him and then covered her breasts.

She was trembling, stiff and tense under his touch, and after a minute he let her go. "What is the matter?" he asked in a puzzled voice.

"I . . . nothing," she answered, bending her head so that her hair swung forward to hide her face.

He put a hand on her shoulder and forced her to turn around. Then he sank down on his heels in front of her. "Did you have a bad experience before?" he asked patiently.

"No." She looked into his brown eyes. "I suppose I shall have to tell you."

"I think you had better."

She looked away from his face down to her tensely clasped hands. "If I am nervous it is because I have never done this before."

"Never done . . . But you were married!"

"It was not a . . . real marriage. Edward never touched me like you just did."

"Good God." He stared at her, clearly stunned by her revelation. "It was *his* idea, this separation?" he said at last.

"Yes! When I married him I did not know . . ."

"Did not know what?" he asked gently as her voice trailed off.

"Edward was not interested in women. Not in that way, at any rate. He married me because he wanted a hostess, a chatelaine, and he wanted to better himself socially. He did not want *me*."

"I see." There was a pause, and then he asked quietly, "Did he like men?"

Laura looked at him in surprise. "How did you know?"

"One sees a bit of that in the navy," he replied a little grimly. Then he asked, "Why didn't you tell your parents? You could have gotten an annulment."

He could see the color slowly rising under her beautiful pale skin, staining her throat and flushing her cheeks and her forehead. "I couldn't," she said a little gruffly. "Edward was very generous to them, you see."

"Yes, I do see," he said quietly after a moment. She found the courage to look up into his face once again. There was an odd expression in his eyes. "I have the strangest wedding nights," he murmured, more to himself than to her.

She didn't say anything, and he reached out to gently smooth her hair back from her face. "Poor Laura. Here I have been thinking all along that you knew the whole game, and you don't even know the first move."

"I am afraid that I don't," she replied in a very small voice.

"Well, we start like this," he said, and drawing her to her feet, he took her in his arms and kissed her. His mouth was gentle, the kiss slow and tender, and after a minute Laura felt herself beginning to relax. He raised his head and laid his cheek against the top of her hair. Her head fit perfectly into the hollow of his shoulder, and she snuggled it there comfortably, her eyes closing in contentment. She felt oddly safe and protected.

"You are so small," he was saying. "It's strange, you don't look small at all, really, but you scarcely come up to my shoulder."

She looked up at that, shyly smiling. "I should imagine everyone must seem small to you, my lord."

He watched her face as she spoke, and his eyes began to glitter between his half-closed lashes. At that look she felt her own breathing alter, but not this time from fear. He slid his hands into her hair and bent to kiss her once again. This time his mouth was hard, asking, demanding a response from her. And she gave it, slipping her arms around his neck so that her breasts were crushed against the hard wall of his chest, opening her mouth for the startling but sweet invasion of his tongue. After a minute, and without letting go of her mouth, he straightened up. Her feet left the floor and he walked with her the few steps necessary to reach the bed. He laid her down and released her only long enough to remove his dressing gown. Then he was beside her again and his hands began to move over her thinly clad body. When he lifted her out of her nightgown, she made no protest, conscious only of his growing urgency and a growing desire in herself to do whatever he asked because only by satisfying him would she find fulfillment for herself.

Laura woke early the next morning as the first light was slanting grayly in through the blinds. She raised herself a little to look down at Mark sleeping beside her. In the early light his relaxed, unguarded face looked very young— as young as he really was. Not for the first time she wondered what it was that had brought that look of still remoteness to his face. He was still deeply asleep, his thick sun-bleached hair ruffled on the pillow like a small boy's. But he was not a small boy, she thought, remembering last night. She lay back against her pillows and regarded the crimson canopy over her. Not a small boy at all.

"Good morning," he said in a soft low voice that sounded to her sensitive ears like a caress. She turned and looked at him.

"Good morning," she replied. And smiled.

He didn't move from where he lay, but put a hand up to gently touch her cheek. She turned her head and kissed his fingers. They did not get up for another hour and a half.

They stayed in London for two weeks, during which time Laura fell in love. She flattered herself that she was getting to know Mark very well. She was touched by his kindness in dealing with Evans, whom he employed to work at Castle Dartmouth as a general estate worker. From the way Evans regarded Mark, she realized that he must have been an excellent officer. "There were hardly ever any floggings on Commander ... Lord Dartmouth's, I mean ... on his lordship's ship," Evans told her in the one conversation she had had with him on the subject. "And the provisions were the best. I mind how he once dumped a whole cargo of rotten food overboard. He was that angry!" said Evans admiringly. "His men would do anything for him."

The few people Mark and Laura saw in London during this time were all naval. They went to a dinner given by Viscount Melville, who was the present First Lord of the Admiralty, and there Laura met a number of the men who had known Mark over the course of his career. She had dressed carefully for the occasion, wanting him to be proud of her, and the warm glow in his eyes when he beheld her in her bronze velvet gown was her reward.

There were no uniforms worn at the dinner, but Laura thought secretly that most of the men present looked as though they ought to be wearing them. It was a revelation to her to see Mark in this company. He looked at home, alert but not wary. And he was obviously held in very high esteem by all these important men.

Captain Sir George Bouden, a gray-haired man in his late forties, was Laura's dinner partner, and after some pleasant talk about the weather and the political situation, he seemed disposed to talk about Mark. Laura encouraged him shamelessly. "I don't know much about this survey," he told her. "Not my line at all, but Dartmouth has always been interested in it. He was always sketching and taking bearings, even when we were in the South Atlantic."

"He is very scientific," said Laura with a smile.

"I don't know about science," replied Sir

George bluntly, "but I will say that I firmly believe he has no equal in the navy in any of the various qualities that constitute a seaman. He is a perfect navigator. A gallant and intelligent leader. An officer who excels in everything that relates to his profession. I'm damn glad to see he's got himself married again, and to a girl like you." He nodded at her approvingly, and Laura felt a little overwhelmed.

"Thank you," she murmured.

"Too many people in this town thrive on gossip," he said abruptly. "Don't you listen to them."

"I have never liked gossip," she said faintly, and wondered what on earth he was referring to. Surely the circumstances of Caroline's suicide had not reached so far as London? Laura had been certain it was only a neighborhood scandal.

After dinner the ladies retired to the drawing room and Laura found herself the object of much curiosity, both covert and overt. The ladies were not as interested in Mark's career as they were in his personal life.

"Such a tragic thing, poor Caroline," Lady Morton said to her as they sat together on a velvet sofa. "I'm afraid everyone rather blamed Dartmouth for it, which was probably most unfair. For a while there it looked as if his career in the navy was finished."

Laura hesitated a moment and then decided not to let this opportunity for information pass. "I had not realized the extent of the damage to his name," she said frankly. "I had thought it was a local matter."

Lady Morton raised a thin, well-bred eyebrow. "Caroline Gregory was the lovliest, most-sought-after girl of the Season," she said. "There were a great number of disappointed young men when she married Dartmouth. And then to hear that that lovely, charming child had killed herself! It was a tremendous shock."

"I see," said Laura slowly. "Was it just the shock . . . or were there other rumors?"

Lady Morton looked at her levelly. "It has just occurred to me that this is hardly the conversation I should be having with Dartmouth's new bride."

"It is rather late to think of that, my lady," said Laura pleasantly. "Were there other rumors?"

"Yes. Oh, nothing terrible, nothing that seventy-five percent of the married men in London don't do. Ignore their wives, I mean, and take a mistress. Only Caroline was such an obvious innocent, so fragilely lovely, so in love, that in her case it seemed very cruel. Especially, of course, in light of what happened."

"I see," Laura said again. She was looking very serious and Lady Morton suddenly reached over and covered her hand.

"I shouldn't have said all that. You see, I knew the Gregorys rather well, and seeing you and Dartmouth together brought it all back. But it is over and finished with, my dear. One shouldn't dwell on the past. It isn't healthy."

At this point there was the sound of men's voices in the saloon and then Lord Melville appeared in the drawing-room doorway. He was talking to Mark. Mark's head was bent toward his host and he was listening gravely, but as he stepped into the room his eyes swept around it quickly, stopping when they came to rest on Laura. She returned his look and it was in that minute that the unsettling and unfamiliar feelings she had been experiencing all week crystallized and she knew she loved him. He said something to Lord Melville, who laughed, and then he was coming across the room toward her with the swift and unwavering gait of a man who is intent on claiming possession.

Laura was only too happy to be claimed, and when, after another hour, he suggested they leave, she took her departure with a prompt obedience that brought a glint of amusement and something else to her husband's eyes.

9

Laura never mentioned her conversation with Lady Morton to Mark, and the second week of their honeymoon went by without any further reminders of the past. The past, it seemed, had buried itself. Mark's reputation, from what Laura could see, could not be brighter. Before they left for Devon, Sir John Barrow, who was the Second Secretary of the Admiralty, asked if he might propose Mark for election to the Royal Society. Mark told her this news in a composed, unemotional voice, but Laura, who was learning to read him, could see that he was very pleased.

They returned to Castle Dartmouth on a cold, windy winter day. The carriage had barely stopped before the front door opened and a small boy dashed out, followed more sedately by the butler and several footmen.

"Laurie! Laurie! Laurie!" Robin shouted, jumping up and down beside the coach. Mark leaned over and opened the door and Robin tumbled in just as the footmen arrived to hand them out. Laura's lap was suddenly full of Robin, who had his arms in a stranglehold around her neck, and she hugged him tightly, pressing her cheek against his bright hair.

"Oh, it's good to see you, darling," she said.

"I missed you," he answered unnecessarily. Then he bounced over to Mark's knees. "I missed you too, Papa."

"You hide your emotions well," his father said with a laugh. "Do you think you might let us get out of this carriage? We are both heartily sick of it, I assure you."

"Of course," said Robin, scrambling out and stepping on Laura's foot in the process.

"Ow!" she yelped, and Mark grinned at her. "You're home," he said.

She gave a little sigh of contentment and allowed the footman to help her out. Lady Maria was standing on the top of the steps by this time, and they all moved toward her, with Robin calling out, again unnecessarily, "Here they are, Aunt Maria!"

After Mark and Laura had divested themselves of their outer wear they all went into the morning parlor, where a big fire was blazing brightly. They ordered tea and Laura sat down in a wing chair with Robin curled at her feet. Lady Maria took the sofa and Mark stood by the chimneypiece. "I have been sitting in that coach for two days now," he said. "It feels good to stand up."

Under cover of the general chatter, Lady Maria carefully studied the faces of the newly married couple. She was pleased by what she saw. Mark looked more relaxed than he had in years, she thought. He looked young again. And Laura—she watched Laura carefully as she was explaining something to Robin and tried to put her finger on what about her was different. She *was* different. There was a difference in the way she held herself, a difference in the look of her eyes. Mark said something teasingly, and she glanced at him for a minute, a slight smile on her lips. Suddenly Lady Maria, who, though she was fifty-five and unmarried, knew something of the world, understood what there was that was different about Laura. A little embarrassed by her own thoughts, she dropped her eyes to her teacup. When she raised them again to reply to something Mark had said, they were perfectly blank. By the time they all arose to go upstairs to change for dinner, Lady Maria was feeling extremely pleased with herself. This marriage had obviously been a brilliant idea, and she took full credit for it.

She remained at Castle Dartmouth for another few weeks. Laura planned to give a dinner party for twenty or so of their closest neighbors, and she asked Lady Maria to stay for it.

"It is not necessary for you to entertain so quickly, my dear," the older woman protested to Laura when the plan had first been mentioned.

"I think it is," replied Laura gravely. "I have received a number of bride visits and I think the sooner everyone sees that Mark and I are a perfectly normal couple with a perfectly normal marriage, the better it will be for us."

She said "better for us," but both of them knew she meant "better for Mark." Lady Maria instantly volunteered to help her goddaughter with the arrangements for the proposed party.

It was the time of year people were to be found in the country, and of the twenty-four people invited, twenty-two accepted. Mark, Laura, and Lady Maria greeted their guests in the drawing room, and when everyone had assembled, they went in to dinner in the state dining room, which was resplendent with precious china, crystal, and silver. Laura faced Mark over the polished table, Lord Countisbury on one side of her and Lord Monksleigh on the other. They were both men whom she had known ever since she first had come to Castle Dartmouth, and she was able to converse with them almost automatically. Her real attention was trained on the other side of the table, where Mark was talking to their wives.

It was during the soup course that Laura noticed she was not the only one in the room who seemed peculiarly aware of Mark, and it was not until dinner was almost over that she realized it was only the women who were so attuned. She puzzled over this for a few minutes and then, as she watched staid Lady Countisbury smile at him girlishly, she knew what the reason was. She shouldn't be so surprised, she told herself ruefully. After all, she had reacted the same way herself. He had the kind of masculine good looks women would always respond to, and when he let his guard drop and his natural charm surface, he could be utterly devastating. She glanced once more around the table and smothered a smile. Everything, she thought, was going to be just fine.

Dinner drew to a close and Laura rose to her feet. Mark, who had hardly glanced at her since the beginning of dinner, rose instantly. "We will leave you gentlemen to your dissipations," she said, and he smiled at her faintly.

"We won't be too long."

Some of the ladies went upstairs to tidy up, and Laura escorted the rest of them into the drawing room. Mrs. Dalton was playing the piano when the men came back into the room. Mark begged her to continue and went himself to stand by the piano. Sir Giles Gregory came over to sit by Laura. She had not seen him in quite some time. He had been away from home when her marriage was suggested, planned, and then concluded. She felt a little nervous about this meeting, but the face she showed to him was one of sweet serenity.

"I don't think I shall ever grow accustomed to calling you Lady Dartmouth," he said gravely.

She averted her eyes from his handsome face and answered lightly, "Then you must continue calling me Laura. You are Robin's uncle, after all. I'm sure Mark would have no objection."

He was silent for a moment, looking at her cameo-clear profile and digesting her words. "And you have given him the right to object, haven't you?" he said at last.

"Yes," she replied simply. She was looking across the room to where her husband stood by the piano. In profile the curve of her eyelashes was very pronounced. There was the faint softness of a smile on her lips.

"Did you marry him for Robin's sake?" Giles asked a little harshly, and at that she turned to look at him. His eyes were deeply blue and she felt a pang of guilt as she read the subdued longing in them.

"Partly," she answered honestly. But she did not want to leave him with the wrong impression. The faint smile on her lips deepened and she said with equal honesty, "And Mark is very hard to resist."

There was a pause, and something flickered behind his eyes. "I know," he said then. "I've seen that before."

Two pairs of blue eyes met and held, Laura's dark and smoky, his clear and brilliant as twin sapphires. "Forget the past, Giles," she said at last. Her voice was very gentle. "We must all of us try now to build for the future. For our own sakes and for the sake of Caroline's son."

After a minute his gaze dropped. He looked suddenly very weary. "I suppose you are right, Laura. I will try."

"Good." She rose from her seat and went over to Lord Countisbury. "Shall we have some cards?" she asked, and at his response, set about organizing the tables.

After they saw the last of the guests off, Lady Maria and Laura looked at each other with quiet triumph. They had been successful. Mark was talking to the butler, and his aunt gestured Laura back into the drawing room, where both ladies collapsed comfortably into chairs.

"I cannot thank you enough, my dear," Lady Maria said sincerely to her goddaughter. "You were splendid. I think we can safely say that the past will trouble us no longer."

"I think it went very well," replied Laura with justifiable complacency. "There was really no feeling of . . . constraint at all."

"No, there was not. Everyone seemed very comfortable."

At that, Mark came into the room. He went to lean his shoulders against the chimneypiece, and both his wife and his aunt regarded his lean length with approval. "I'm afraid our neighbors fall into the category of worthy but dull," he said blandly to those satisfied faces.

Both his wife and his aunt bristled. "Not everyone wants to spend the whole evening talking about science or archaeology," snapped Lady Maria.

"You certainly gave the impression you were enjoying yourself," Laura said accusingly. "My goodness, by the end of the night you had Lady Countisbury eating out of your hand!"

He raised an ironic eyebrow. "I thought that was the whole point of the evening," he said.

There was a stunned silence and the two women exchanged a glance. They had not known Mark was aware of their motives. His look of irony deepened and he said dryly, "I'm not blind."

"Well, that is nice to know," his aunt retorted vigorously, recovering her equilibrium. "And let me tell you, young man, you had better learn to appreciate the virtues of men like Lord Countisbury." She went on to discourse largely on the local Dartmouth gentry and he listened and watched her with amused tolerance. And Laura watched him.

It had been quite deliberate, then, that apparently effortless charming of his women guests this evening. She had thought it unconscious. For the first time she realized that he was quite capable of exploiting his physical magnetism and clever enough to do it so that no one saw through him. It was, she thought, a disquieting discovery to make about one's husband.

10

The winter months of January and February went by, and Mark was deeply involved in work on his charts. Often he would spend eight to ten hours at a time in the library. His correspondence with prominent antiquarians, travelers, and scholars increased in volume, and Laura several times found herself entertaining a single male guest who would closet himself with Mark for hours in the library, appearing only for dinner.

She was very proud of her husband. The reality of this intense, brilliant, guarded young man had swept out of her mind all the other men she had ever known. She felt so alive when she was with him. She loved their after-dinner talks in the drawing room. He was so interesting, so interested in everything. Talking to him was like setting out on a new and exciting road which kept opening up new paths here and there as they progressed along. Her mind felt stretched, as it had never done before.

At the end of February he was elected to the Royal Society, Britain's most prestigious scientific club, and went up to London for a few weeks to meet his fellow members. He asked Laura if she wanted to come with him, but she felt she would only be a nuisance. She was always afraid to presume too much with him; she was acutely conscious that their marriage had not been made for love. The fact that she had fallen in love with him did not mean he had done the same with her. He desired her, she certainly knew that, but she was adult enough to realize that a man could desire where he did not love.

And so when he said diffidently, "Should you care to come with me?" she refused.

"I would only be in your way, Mark. You are dying to submerge yourself in talk about new instruments and how to measure wind and how to predict storms, and all the other ideas your mind is teeming with. You don't want to have to worry about me."

"And *you* will be happier here with Robin."

"I didn't say that."

"No, you are far too tactful and discreet to say that." He smiled a little crookedly. "But you meant it, all the same."

They were together in the schoolroom, where Mark had come to find her with the news of his election. And they were alone; Robin had gone down to Laura's room to fetch a book she had forgotten. He put his hands now on her shoulders. "My tactful, thoughtful, considerate wife," he murmured. "Are you certain you won't change your mind and come? I'm certain I can think of something that would entertain you while we're there."

Laura's heart began to accelerate and her lids came down on her eyes under the look in his. "Laura?" he said very softly, and she looked up. His eyes were as golden brown as fine sherry and had the same dizzying effect on her. She loved him so much it hurt.

"Papa!" said Robin's voice from behind them. "Have you come to see my castle? I built it myself."

Mark let Laura go and turned to his bright-eyed son. "I came to see Laurie, but now that I'm here, I should love to see your castle."

Laura watched approvingly as the two of them got down on the floor to allow Robin to demonstrate his new treasure. She remarked, as she had several times before, that Mark never lied to Robin, even about little things like coming to see him instead of her. He seemed always to see Robin as an individual person in his own right, not just an appendage or offshoot of himself. He respected Robin. It was not the usual way of parents toward their children, and Laura admired his attitude very much. Robin had grown up a great deal since Mark had come home.

He stayed for about fifteen minutes and then said, "Well, Farnsworth has been after me to go and look at a new drainage ditch, and today is a good day for it, I suppose. The sun is finally out."

"May I come too, Papa?" asked Robin eagerly.

Mark looked at Laura. "Only if it won't be interrupting your lessons."

"No." Laura shook her head. "Take him along if you like."

"Very well," Mark said to his son. "Change into riding clothes and meet me in the hall in fifteen minutes."

"All right!" said Robin, and dashed for the door leading to his bedroom.

Fifteen minutes later Laura watched as father and son walked down the front steps of Castle Dartmouth toward the horse and pony awaiting them on the drive. Robin was holding his head exactly as Mark held his, and Laura smiled to see them. Of late Robin had become a very faithful imitator of "my papa." Laura thought he could choose no better model.

She did not go to London with Mark, even though she would have liked to do so. She thought she would be in his way, and when she told him once again of her reason, he did not press her. His easy acquiescence in her refusal only confirmed her belief in her own superfluity.

He was gone for two weeks, during which time Laura's outward existence seemed remarkably unchanged. They had not engaged a governess for Robin. "In another year he will be ready for a tutor," Laura had said to Mark. "I can certainly teach him until then. I enjoy it. And when I am occupied, he is very well-supervised by Betty or Rose. There is no need for a governess at this point."

Mark had agreed, and so life for Laura continued in almost the same pattern as it had before her marriage. She spent the mornings in the schoolroom with Robin, teaching him to read and to do simple mathematics, and in the afternoon she rode or went into Dartmouth on errands or visited with her neighbors. She was active in several local charities, particularly the area orphanage, which she visited regularly every week. It was a simple, tranquil country life, full of small pleasures, like choosing the flowers she wanted from the garden or discussing with the rector how best to assist the local families who were suffering from the postwar economy. It was a life that suited Laura very well. She liked serenity. She liked to spend whole afternoons fishing or gardening. She was perfectly content to get her excitement out of jumping her horse over the ha-ha.

Marriage to Mark had not changed her life in any outward way. She still had Robin, her friends, her occupations. It was, then, a little disconcerting to find herself missing him so much during the weeks of his absence. Outwardly her days might not have changed, but inwardly she had changed very much. Her husband had become the focal point of her emotional life. She might not see him often during the day, but she was aware of him nonetheless, aware of his presence behind the library door, aware that he was out somewhere on the estate and might return at any minute, aware that at any time the schoolroom or morning-parlor door might open and he would be there. She missed that faint feeling of expectancy that hung over her all day when he was home. She missed seeing him sitting across from her at dinner, missed their after-dinner discussions in the drawing room. She missed him at night as she lay in her big lonely bed. She longed quite desperately for him to come home.

Her hidden life, however, remained hidden, and those who surrounded her never suspected that she was not perfectly content be her husband present or absent. A few days before Mark was due to return, Giles Gregory rode over to see Robin and to talk to Laura. They had not seen him in almost a month, as he had been making a round of visits to the country homes of several of his friends. As one of the most desirable bachelors in London, Giles always had plenty of invitations.

He had several new puzzles for Robin, one of which was a map of Britain, and the two of them sat doing it for almost an hour. Then Giles came downstairs to have tea with Laura.

It was a blowy March day and they sat in front of the fire in the yellow saloon, which was the room Laura used most often. It was bright and sunny with its yellow walls and draperies and upholstery, and it always cheered her up on a dark, depressing day. "How are the Marchbanks?" she asked Giles demurely. Laura had met this aristocratic couple and their daughter when they had come to stay with Lord and Lady Monksleigh.

"On the hunt," he replied ruefully, looking over the plate of cakes on the table beside him.

Unobserved, Laura looked hard at his face. He was an extraordinarily good-looking man, with hair like Robin's and eyes that were even bluer. He was in his early thirties, she estimated. Time he was getting married. "Why don't you allow yourself to get caught?" she asked bluntly. "Lady Anne seemed a very nice girl."

He selected a cake with great care and balanced it neatly between long fingers. "She doesn't appeal to me," he said at last. His voice was very calm. "I lost the only girl I ever cared about . . . but, then, you know all about that."

There was a pause and then Laura said firmly, "If she is lost, then you must look around for someone to take her place."

"Do you think so?"

"Yes, I do, Giles."

There was quiet as he ate his cake and she sipped her tea, and then, changing the subject, he said, "Robin tells me Mark is in London."

"Yes. He was elected to the Royal Society." She couldn't quite keep the pride out of her voice, and he regarded her thoughtfully.

"That's quite an honor," he murmured. "Who proposed him?"

Laura had received a letter from Mark only that morning, and she was dying to tell someone. "Sir John Barrow, from the Admiralty, was going to propose him, but when Mark's name came up, the President, Sir Joseph Banks, said that Sir John's sponsorship was unnecessary. He told Sir John that Mark had no need for favor of any kind but would come amongst them on his own sole account, as he ought to without owing thanks to anyone." Her face was now aglow with pride. "He was elected unanimously, so highly regarded is he by his peers."

"So it seems," said Giles, his eyebrows raised a little. Then he smiled. "I'm glad, Laura. Glad that things are going well for you and for Mark."

She met his smiling blue eyes and felt a rush of gratitude toward him. He was behaving very well. Really, she didn't quite know how she had resisted him for all those years. Perhaps, she thought with a sudden flash of intuition, it was because he reminded her of Edward. "Thank you, Giles. And remember what I said, will you? It's time you had a son of your own, not just a nephew."

"I'll think about it," was all he would say in return.

Four days later Mark came home. Laura was out, as he had not sent her word of his exact arrival date. It was a warm sunny day, the sort of day that truly promised spring, and she had decided to ride her horse in to see the rector rather than take the carriage. She came home by her favorite route, cutting off the main road to turn in toward the huge Castle Dartmouth park. Mark's father had long ago pulled down the wall that enclosed this part of his property and had had a ha-ha dug. The invisible sunken ditch was considered more natural-looking than a wall. When she came this way, Laura, who was an excellent horsewoman, had two stiles to jump as well as the ha-ha, which was banked here, making the jump more difficult.

She was flushed with exercise when she reached the house. A footman came down the front stairs to take her horse in charge, and the butler met her at the door with the news that "My lord arrived an hour ago, my lady."

Laura's expression did not change, but indefinably, she began to glow. "Oh, good. Where is he, Monk?"

"I believe he is in the schoolroom with Master Robin, my lady."

She nodded her thanks to the servant and proceeded up the great open staircase with disciplined and sedate steps—disciplined because she felt an overwhelming desire to run. When she pushed open the schoolroom door she saw the two heads bent close together over a book on the table. At the sound of her entrance the blond and the brown head turned with an identical gesture. "Papa's back, Laurie!" Robin said. "He brought me a book of maps—a Natlas. Come and see."

"Atlas, darling," she responded, and moved forward. "How nice to have you home, Mark," she said composedly, and offered him her cheek to kiss.

He touched it with his lips. "How are you, Laura? Been out enjoying the spring weather, I see."

"Yes. I was over to visit the rector."

"Look at my book, Laurie," Robin demanded, and obediently she bent her head to do so. They remained in the schoolroom for another twenty minutes, talking to each other and to the child, their manners pleasant and civilized. Then Robin asked Mark if he would play bat and ball with him in the garden, and Mark agreed. Robin came back into the house an hour later, but Laura did not see Mark again until dinner.

Over dinner he told her about his trip to London and about some of the men he had met. Then he asked what she had been doing in his absence.

"Oh, the same things I have been doing for years," she responded with a deprecatory smile. "Just at present I am organizing the Easter party for the children at the orphanage. Do you mind if we use the grounds here?"

"Of course I don't mind. What are you planning?"

"Oh, games and contests, that sort of thing. And quantities of food, of course. We've done it every year, but at the orphanage, not here. I think it would be nice for the children to have a change of scene for the day."

"Yes." He looked at her steadily across the table. She had dressed with special care that evening, choosing a gown that left more of her neck and shoulders bare than usual. They shimmered in the candlelight, luminous and white against the deep blue of her gown. Her eyes looked very dark from where he sat. "Yes," he repeated. "It would be nice for them. You might use the ballroom to serve the food. April can be chilly."

"What a good idea. Thank you, darling. The rector will be so pleased." She looked down at her plate and then carefully put down her fork. That "darling" had slipped out unintentionally. She looked up to find him still watching her. It was the look that could always make her heart swim.

"This sort of life suits you, doesn't it?" he asked. "Or are you secretly pining for the excitement of London?"

"Not at all," she replied with outward calm. "I like my garden, my charities, my neighbors, my boy. I like making a home." For you, she added silently. I like making a home for you. But she did not say that. She loved him but she was afraid to tell him so. She did not know if he would want to hear it. The problem was, she was not, she could not be, sure of him.

"I'm happy to hear that," he replied, and there was absolutely no expression in his voice. "It seems our marriage was a good idea after all."

"For me it was," she replied quietly.

He looked at her in silence for a minute and then he smiled. She was conscious again of his magnetism, his charm. He could do it so effortlessly, she thought, turn her heart upside down like this. And he knew he was doing it, too—that was the trouble. He stood up. "Come upstairs and I'll show you how I feel about it," he said softly.

She didn't reply, but allowed him to take her arm and escort her upstairs to her bedroom.

11

The good weather held, and three days later Mark suggested Laura and Robin accompany him on an expedition to Dartmouth Castle. It had come out in conversation the previous night that Laura had never been in it.

"You must let me give you a tour," Mark said. "If you are a Cheney, you must see the castle. It is worth seeing, you know. Parts of it go back to Norman times. It has a square tower from the time of Edward IV and a round tower from the time of Henry VII. My grandfather was perfectly correct when he decided it was not a comfortable residence, but we have always kept it in repair, even after the family moved to Castle Dartmouth. It's one of the main historic landmarks of Devon, not to mention its importance in the history of my own family."

It was a bright, mild afternoon when Laura and Mark, with Robin squeezed in between them on the seat of the phaeton, set off for

Dartmouth Castle. As they bowled along in the clear March sun, they looked to be exactly what they were: a happy, affectionate family group. Many weeks later Laura was to look back on this moment with wild longing and despair. But for now she was happy. Mark, dressed in a russet coat, buckskins, and polished top boots, looked relaxed and even allowed Robin to hold the reins for a brief moment as they went down a wide and deserted stretch of the road. Robin was simply ecstatic; he was thrilled to be going out with them, thrilled to be up in the phaeton, and speechless at being allowed to hold the reins.

The castle was truly impressive. Laura had seen its outside many times; anyone who visited Dartmouth could scarcely help that. It dominated the town and the river, whose waters flowed right past its walls. Walking through its great stone chambers and towers was to travel back hundreds of years in time. Mark was an excellent tour guide, and both Laura and Robin trailed after him, fascinated, asking questions and hanging on his every reply.

Then Mark mentioned a magic word and Robin's entire small body quivered with delight. "Dungeons? Did you say dungeons, Papa?"

Mark looked at his son and grinned. "Only a few small cells down at the level of the river. There are no torture chambers, Robin, I regret to say."

"But they are *dungeon* cells?" Robin asked urgently.

"Yes. At least they are certainly cold and damp and dark enough to qualify for that label."

"May I see them?" Robin was tugging at Mark's arm in his excitement.

"I suppose so." His father ruffled his hair affectionately. "They smell, too," he added.

Robin heaved an ecstatic sigh, and Laura laughed. "Do *you* want to see the dungeons?" Mark asked her, a note of amusement in his own voice.

"No, thank you," she replied firmly. "Cold, damp, dark, smelly places have no appeal for me."

"Laurie!"

"I'm sorry, Robin. I know it's poor-spirited of me, but there it is. You and Papa can go alone."

"I'm afraid ladies are like that, Robin," Mark said gravely.

"Well, this lady certainly is," she returned spiritedly.

He relented. "Very well, Robin and I will investigate the dungeons by ourselves. If you'd like to go up to the North Tower, Laura, you'll get a splendid view of the surrounding countryside."

"Now, that sounds more appealing. How do I get there?"

He pointed the way, and he and Robin turned back down the stairs as Laura moved off in the opposite direction. She poked along for a while, looking into deserted bedrooms, until at last she found herself in the tower room Mark had mentioned. There was a stone balcony outside the archway that had once held a door, and she stepped outside for a better look. Mark had been right when he said the view was splendid. Laura could see for miles, and she amused

herself by trying to pick out familiar landmarks from this unaccustomed height.

She was turning to go back into the tower
room when she heard Mark calling her. His
voice was coming from the courtyard directly
below the balcony, and she leaned out from the
stone parapet to call back to him. There was a
dreadful grinding sound and then Laura felt
the stone against which she was leaning her
whole weight give way beneath her. She was
falling, and screamed as she blindly reached
out for something to grab on to. There was
nothing.

It was her cloak that saved her. When she
had turned back to the parapet to answer Mark,
the full wool cloak had swung out and over the
carved stone figures that adorned the side
parapet. When Laura pitched forward, the cloak
caught, and for just a few seconds held her
back, so that instead of following the crashing
stone to the courtyard sixty feet below, she
was left with the lower half of her body flat on
the stone floor while from the waist up she
dangled forward into space.

Sheer terror kept her still for a minute, and
then she heard Mark shout, "Don't move, Laura!
Stay perfectly still! I'm coming."

For what seemed hours she lay there, afraid
that if she tried to inch her way backward she
would either unbalance herself and fall forward or that the stone beneath her would give
way as the parapet had. Then, after an eternity,
she felt Mark's hands grasp her ankles. "I have
you, Laura." His voice was calm and quiet. "I'm

going to pull you backward now. I don't know how safe this balcony is, so we'll go slowly."

Her body moved along the stone, and slowly she was pulled up from her precariously dangling position over the courtyard. Then his hands were around her waist and he lifted her off the balcony entirely and into the safety of the tower room and his arms.

She was shivering uncontrollably and pressed against him as if he were the only shelter in a nightmare world. The arms holding her to him were like iron bands. "It's all right," he kept repeating over and over. "You're safe now, love. It's all right."

From a long way away they could hear a small, near-to-hysterical voice crying, "Papa! Papa! Where are you?"

"Here, Robin," Mark called strongly, and his arms loosened a little from around Laura. With tremendous effort she took her head out of his shoulder.

"You'd better get him," she said shakily.

"Are you all right?"

She swallowed and stepped back from him. "Yes."

"Papa!" came the scream again.

"I'll be right back," Mark said to her, and she could hear him running down the narrow staircase, calling Robin's name. He was back very quickly, and a frightened Robin ran across the room and into her arms.

"It's all right, Robin darling," she said, her turn now to hold someone tight and speak words of reassurance. "Papa got me. I'm perfectly safe." Robin began to cry, and she held him close to her while Mark walked over to look out at the damaged balcony. He said something very quietly, and Laura looked nervously down at the bright head that was pressed to her breast. She hoped fervently that Robin hadn't heard him.

The mood on the ride home was far from the happy expectancy of the earlier trip. Reaction had hit Laura and she felt utterly exhausted. There was a distinctly grim look about Mark's well-cut mouth, but he was quiet, concentrating on his driving. It was not until they turned into the gates of the park that he said, "I'll find out directly who is responsible for maintenance at the castle. It was inexcusable that that balcony should have been left like that."

"It really was not at all visible," Laura said tiredly. "It was only when I leaned against it that the rotten stone gave way. I don't think it was anyone's fault, Mark."

"It was inexcusable," he said again, and something in his level voice caught her attention. It took her a minute to realize that he was in a quiet, deadly rage. "You might have been killed," he said.

"Yes. But it was an accident."

He did not reply, but pulled up in front of the house. As a footman came down the steps toward them, he said, "You and Robin go in, Laura. I will take the phaeton down to the stables."

She heard later, from her butler, that Mark had fired the two men who were responsible for keeping Dartmouth Castle in repair.

12

Laura determined to put all thoughts of the accident out of her mind, and being a girl with basically good nerves, she was largely successful. She never mentioned the incident to anyone at all, and when Lady Monksleigh asked her about it a week later, she was taken by surprise. Her ladyship had come to Castle Dartmouth to talk to Laura about a ball the Monksleighs were planning for the end of April, and the two women were sitting in the morning parlor having tea.

"What is this story I hear about you nearly falling to your death over at Dartmouth Castle?" Lady Monksleigh asked, stirring some sugar into her cup.

Laura looked startled. "However did you hear about that, Louisa?"

"My dear, how does anyone hear about anything? The servants, of course. One of the men Dartmouth sacked is the brother of a man who works for us."

Laura smiled ruefully. "Oh, dear. That's what comes of living in the country, I suppose."

"London is worse," Lady Monksleigh said simply. "But tell me, what happened?"

"I was leaning against the stone parapet on one of the tower balconies and it gave way. I almost fell after it into the courtyard, but luckily my cloak got caught. Mark pulled me to safety." Laura put down her teacup. "It was frightful, Louisa, and I'd really rather not talk about it."

"My dear, how dreadful. I don't blame you at all. I should have been simply hysterical."

There was a moment's silence and Laura picked up her cup again and began to sip from it. Lady Monksleigh said, "Mason, the man whom Dartmouth fired, has been telling everyone that it was not his fault. He swears there was nothing wrong with the stone when he was there last week."

Laura bit her lip. "I feel sorry for him," she confessed. "Really, Louisa, there was no way one could tell the stone was rotten. But Mark was furious. He wouldn't listen. He simply got very white about the mouth and said I might have been killed and it was inexcusable. I do hope the poor men can get other jobs."

"I expect they will," Lady Monksleigh said placidly. She did not share Laura's interest in the area unemployment problem. She was, however, extremely interested in her noble neighbors, and by the end of two weeks every person of Laura's acquaintance had heard about her accident.

"My poor girl, what a terrifying experience,"

Giles Gregory said to her when he came to visit Robin five days after Lady Monksleigh's visit. As Laura had already been condoled with by the rector, Mrs. Dalton, and Lady Countisbury, she was heartily sick of the subject.

"It *was* terrifying and I should like to forget it," she replied tartly. "However, that is difficult to do when every person I talk to insists on bringing the topic up."

He looked a little taken aback. "I'm sorry. I didn't realize it was such a touchy subject."

She felt a little ashamed of herself. "I didn't mean to snap at you, Giles. But, truly, I would rather not talk about it."

He scanned her face with narrowed eyes and then suddenly smiled. "I understand. Now, tell me, how are the arrangements for the Easter party coming along?"

She smiled back at him gratefully. "Very well, thank you. I have ordered the prizes from Melville's, and . . ."

They were still talking comfortably half an hour later when the door opened and Mark came in. He looked a little surprised to see Giles but shook hands pleasantly enough when his former brother-in-law stood up. Giles did not remain for long after Mark's arrival, and after he had donned hat and coat and gone on his way, Mark turned to his wife. "It seems to me that fellow is here rather often," he said. "And for the whole afternoon, too. I saw his carriage down at the stable two hours ago."

"He comes to see Robin," Laura said composedly. "They are awfully fond of one another."

He raised an eyebrow in a way that clearly

suggested skepticism. "Are you sure it's *Robin* he comes to see?"

Faint color flushed into her cheeks. "Of course. It's only natural that he be attached to his nephew, Mark. Robin is all the family poor Giles has." Immediately the words were out of her mouth, Mark's face changed: the visor came down, the mask of cool indifference which he assumed whenever anything associated with his former wife was mentioned. Laura could have kicked herself for her thoughtless words. She was usually so careful with him on that topic. The problem was that she felt slightly guilty about Giles and so had neglected her usual caution.

"True," he said coolly. "That probably explains it."

She wanted to reach out her arms to him, to comfort whatever terrible hurt it was that made him look like that, but she knew she could not. She was utterly certain that he would reject any such overture on her part, and she didn't think she could bear to be rejected by him. So she only replied helplessly, "Yes, I think it does."

She went up to bed early that night and was half-sitting, half-lying against her pillows reading a book when Mark came through the connecting door between their rooms. He smiled faintly when he saw her and crossed the floor saying, "Didn't your nurse ever tell you it was bad for your posture to read like that?"

She closed her book. "We all need to have *some* vice," she said. "Mine is reading in bed."

He sat down on the edge of the bed beside her and took the book from her unresisting hand. He looked at the title and his lips pursed a little in surprise. "Hardly what one would call relaxing bedtime reading," he said, looking at his own copy of Adam Smith's *Wealth of Nations*.

She smiled. "It isn't quite *Housewifely Remedies*," she agreed.

He put the book on the bedside table, then reached out to run gentle fingers across her cheekbone, down her jaw and the long slender column of her neck. His touch had its usual devastating effect on her, and she gazed up at him, utterly still under his hand. He began to undo the small pearl buttons of her nightgown, and then, when he had finished, looked for a moment in silence at the bared silk of her beautiful body. "All this, and brains too." He leaned forward to kiss her throat, her breasts. "You're too good to be true, Laura," he murmured.

She slid her fingers into his thick hair. "Mark ..." Her voice was husky, and hearing it, he raised his head and found her mouth. It opened under his immediately, sweet and yielding, answering to his desire and hunger with the promise that whatever he might want, he would find it here, in her arms.

Later, lying awake while he slept peacefully beside her, Laura thought of the strange double life she had been leading these last few months. During the day she felt she had the marriage she had expected—a marriage of civility, of conformity, of mutual respect for one another's privacy. But at night, when he came to her like this, then she felt they were truly lovers, truly two people who needed each other and who fulfilled each other. Without him, she felt, she would be only half a person, a rudderless empty vessel scudding aimlessly down the river of her life.

But Mark? Did he feel like that about her? When he held her and whispered love words to her and caressed her with such erotic tenderness, then she felt he did. But was it Laura he turned to like this? Did he come to *her*? Or did he come merely to find the transformation of the world a man always seeks in the body of a woman? She did not know.

He stirred a little beside her, as if aware of her disturbed thoughts, and she turned to look down at him. The lamplight fell on his face, young and defenseless-looking in sleep. He was not defenseless, however, she thought a little painfully. The problem was that his defenses were all too effective.

Hers were not. Her eyes moved from his face down to his bare, leanly muscled chest and broad strong shoulders. He moved again, and in his sleep his hand came into contact with her bare arm. She closed her eyes. No. Against him she had no defenses at all.

During the next few weeks Laura was extremely busy planning the orphanage Easter party. The early-spring weather was cold but clear and sunny, and she took to using Mark's phaeton on her trips to and from the shops in town and the vicarage. Laura drove extremely well. Better than he did, Mark told her admiringly after driving out with her one afternoon.

"Well, I don't imagine you have had much chance to practice," she said in response to his comment.

"True. A life at sea rather restricts one from developing one's horsemanship. You will have to uphold the family honors in that department."

They were coming back from Dartmouth, where Laura had been to the shops and Mark to see Retired Admiral Falsey, who lived in the town. Laura negotiated a particularly difficult turn with misleading ease and said, "Nonsense. You are a very good driver. You ride well, too." The tiniest of mischievous smiles pulled at the corner of her mouth. "For a sailor," she added.

He chuckled. "Thank you . . . I think. Shall I propose you for the Four-Horse Club? I understand that is *the* prestigious organization for the horsey set."

"First of all, they would never let me join because I am a woman. Second, I shouldn't want to even if they would. They wear the most dreadful outfit, I hear. And third, you sounded odiously condescending when you said 'horsey set.'" She imitated his voice as she said the last words and contrived to look down her elegantly straight nose.

"Would you describe that tone as odiously condescending?" he asked with interest. "It was the way you said 'for a sailor,' which I was endeavoring to reproduce."

She laughed. "Touché, you wretch."

They drove for a few more minutes in silence and then he asked, "Do you hunt, Laura?"

"I used to hunt when I lived at home. I haven't done much lately, I'm afraid."

"Why?"

"Oh . . . one reason or another," she answered lightly. The fact was, she had not wanted to buy several expensive hunters and stable them at Castle Dartmouth. Before Mark had come home, the stables had been empty except for her hack, Robin's pony, and two carriage horses. They had not had the staff to look after any additional horses.

"Do you *like* to hunt?" he asked insistently.

"I adore it," she confessed.

"Well, we shall have to get you some horses, then. There is plenty of room in the stables. Certainly you must hunt this winter, since you like it so much."

She was silent for a minute and then she said quietly, "Thank you, Mark. I should like that. But I should like it even better if I were busy doing something else this winter."

Her eyes were on the road in front of her, so she did not see his look of surprise. "Oh? And what is that?"

"Having a baby," she replied. When he didn't say anything, she went on, her voice almost too steady, "Are you very disappointed that nothing has happened yet?"

"Disappointed? Of course not!" He sounded astonished that she could think such a thing. But Laura was acutely conscious that having more children was one of the reasons he had given for marrying her. And she had just had depressing evidence this morning that she was definitely not pregnant. Maybe next month. . . .

"Anyway," she said with an attempt at lightness, "I think I shall hold off buying horses for a while. I do very much want to have a baby."

"I'm trying, Laura," he said humorously, "I'm trying." She turned to find him laughing at her. For some reason, she felt immeasurably better.

"I know. I've been so impressed by your sense of duty, my lord." She cast him a quick look out of the corner of her eye.

"Have you indeed?" he said dangerously. "If you weren't driving this phaeton, I'd give you something to be impressed with."

Laura raised her hands and the horses increased their speed. "Don't distract me," she said smartly. "You don't want to have an accident, do you?"

He leaned back in his seat. "I'm certain you are far too skillful to have an accident, my love," he said smoothly.

"I hope so," she replied, unaccountably warmed by the endearment, even if he was only teasing her.

13

It seemed, however, that Laura was not to avoid the accident she had threatened Mark with. And it happened, ironically, the day after their conversation about it.

It was Holy Thursday, and the orphanage Easter party was scheduled for Saturday. Laura was supervising the preparation of the ballroom for the serving of refreshments; she did not wish to ask the servants to work extra on Good Friday. Maria Dalton and Giles Gregory stopped by for a few minutes during the course of the morning to ask if they could assist her, but Laura had things well in hand.

"I'm going to drive over to see the rector later. He has all the children's pictures for the art contest. I'll bring them back and we'll hang them over there." She gestured to a large board some workmen were erecting between two of the windows. "I've got Lady Countisbury to judge the art and award the ribbon," she said with some complacency.

Giles raised his eyebrows. "I'm impressed. Should you like me to get the pictures for you?"

"No, thank you, Giles. I've a few things to discuss with Dr. Norris. I'll get them."

It was about three in the afternoon when Laura left for the parsonage. The sky had clouded up and she was conscious of a hope that the weather, which had been so unusually good of late, would at least hold until Saturday. She was driving briskly down the road toward the parsonage when she saw a gig approaching along the road from the opposite direction. She shortened her reins a little and pulled her horses toward the side of the road. The next thing she knew, the phaeton tilted sharply, turned over, and she was thrown from her high seat into the ditch at the side of the road.

She lay still, stunned, the breath knocked out of her. Then, dimly, she heard a voice calling, "Lady Dartmouth! Are you all right? Can you hear me? Lady Dartmouth!"

She opened her eyes and saw an unfamiliar face bending over her. "What happened?" she asked faintly.

"The wheel came off your carriage, my lady. Are you all right? Can you sit up?"

"Yes, I think so." She was lying half on her side, half on her back, and when she tried to push herself up, a flash of pain went through her left shoulder. "Oh . . ." she gasped.

"Let me help you," came the strange man's voice.

"Yes, please." Two strong hands took hold of her, and in a moment she was on her feet. She swayed for a minute and the hands held her firmly. Her vision steadied and she said, "I'm all right now. Thank you." She looked up and recognized Robert Bertram, an independent farmer who lived not far from Castle Dartmouth. "Why, Mr. Bertram. I didn't recognize you at first."

"I don't wonder," he said a trifle grimly. "That was a nasty accident, my lady."

"Hi, there!" came a cry from the road. "What's happened? Why ... Lady Dartmouth!" It was Lord Monksleigh, on horseback and alone. Laura and Mr. Bertram were still down in the ditch and Lord Monksleigh dismounted and came over to take hold of Laura's horses, which were growing extremely restless.

"Lady Dartmouth's carriage lost a wheel, my lord, and she was thrown." The broadly built, ruddy-faced farmer turned to Laura. "Do you think you can climb up the side of this ditch, my lady?"

"Of course," she replied, and took a step forward. Her legs shook. Without a word, the burly farmer picked her up and carried her up the rise.

"Thank you, Mr. Bertram," Laura said as he put her gently on her feet.

Both men looked at her worriedly. She was very pale. Her tan pelisse was filthy from the ditch, and her long hair had come out of its neat chignon.

"Laura," said Lord Monksleigh, forgetting formality, "go and sit in Bertram's carriage. As soon as we unharness your horses we'll take you home."

Laura nodded, and Mr. Bertram, who was getting more exercise than he had bargained for that day, lifted her up to the seat of his gig. The single horse that was drawing it, a cob, stood quietly as he had all along.

Mr. Bertram went back to Lord Monksleigh, and the two men proceeded to unharness the horses. Then Mr. Bertram went to look at the wheel. "My lord," he said in a curious voice, "will you come and look at this for a minute?"

Lord Monksleigh gave the horses to Bertram to hold and looked. He didn't say anything, but when he straightened up, his face was very grave. "Yes, I see what you mean Bertram." Both men turned to look at Laura, and Lord Monksleigh lowered his voice. "Don't say anything to Lady Dartmouth. Drive her home and send someone back here for the horses. I'll have a word with her husband about the phaeton later."

"Very good, my lord," said Mr. Bertram tonelessly. Both men glanced once again, involuntarily, toward the damaged wheel, and then the farmer went over to mount his gig to drive Laura home. What neither man told her was that the shaft that held the wheel had been very neatly sawed through.

Mark was working in the library when Robert Bertram escorted Laura up the steps of Castle Dartmouth, to be admitted by a very concerned butler. A footman ran to summon him, and he was in the front hall before Laura had her pelisse off. "What happened?" he asked sharply, and Laura turned to him with obvious relief.

"Oh, Mark!" Monk had her coat in his hands by now, and she half-ran the few steps that separated her from her husband and buried her face in his shoulder. Automatically his arms came up to hold her, but he looked at Robert Bertram.

"What happened?" he repeated.

"The wheel came off Lady Dartmouth's phaeton and she was thrown into the ditch, my lord," said the wooden-faced farmer.

Mark's own face became very still. "I see," he said quietly.

"I left Lord Monksleigh attending to the horses, my lord. Perhaps you might send someone to assist him?"

"Of course." Mark glanced at his butler. "Attend to it, Monk."

"Yes, my lord."

Laura took her face out of her husband's shoulder. "Mr. Bertram has been so kind, Mark. He rescued me from the ditch and drove me home."

Mark inclined his head. "I am much obliged to you, Bertram. May I offer you some refreshment?"

"No, thank you, my lord. I'll leave you to see to her ladyship. She had a nasty fall; it's fortunate she wasn't seriously hurt." Robert Bertram did not smile as he said, "Good day to you, my lord," and took his leave.

When they were alone in the hall, Mark said to Laura, "What you need first is a glass of wine to put some color back into your cheeks."

"Perhaps you're right," she said with a shaky laugh, and allowed him to guide her into the library.

The wine did help. When she had finished the glass, she put her hand up and for the first time realized that her hair had come down. "Good heavens," she said faintly, "I must look a fright."

He smiled for the first time since she had come in. "You must be feeling better if you are beginning to worry about your appearance."

"I need a bath." She rose to her feet and involuntarily winced as her bruises made themselves known.

"Are you all right?" he asked quickly.

"Just bruised and sore, I think. Nothing's broken."

"Shall I summon the doctor?"

"No, truly, Mark, I am all right. All I need is a bath and some fresh clothes."

"I'll come upstairs with you," he said, and watched her carefully as she walked beside him, slowly but steadily. He didn't leave her until her maid had arrived and the tub before the fire was being filled with hot water.

He went back downstairs, intending to return to the library, and was informed that Lord Monksleigh was in the Chinese saloon and desired to talk to him. Mark walked to the designated room, a look of guarded remoteness on his unusually white face.

The Easter party for the orphanage children was a great success, at least from the children's point of view. There were all sorts of races and competitions held on the magnificent south lawn of Castle Dartmouth. There were pony rides. There was a magician. And, set up in the sumptuous Italian ballroom of the house, there was enough food to feed an army, let alone a troop of little boys and girls.

A surprising number of Laura's wellborn neighbors attended as well. Maria Dalton had always been interested in the orphanage, but Lady Monksleigh and Lady Countisbury had taken it up only recently. It was, they had decided, the fashionable thing to do. These ladies had brought along their husbands, the rector was there with his wife, and Sir Giles Gregory was also present.

Laura was too busy with the children to pay much attention to her neighbors. They had all been given ceremonial functions, but she hardly expected much in the way of actual assistance from the baronesses or their husbands. Maria Dalton and Giles were in charge of the food, and Laura, the rector, and Mark ran the games on the lawn. All the workers were so involved with the children that they scarcely had a chance to speak to each other. Laura herself did not even sit down until all the children were sitting around tables in the ballroom, stuffing food into themselves with astonishing rapidity.

"Good heavens," she said to Mark as she collapsed into an empty chair next to him. "The older boys have finished already! One would think they hadn't been fed for weeks.

And the food at the orphanage is quite good, really."

Mark looked with her toward the two tables of restless boys. Then he looked around his priceless ballroom. "I'll take them outside," he said promptly, and rose to his feet. The boys looked positively ecstatic as he collected them and herded them out the door with the promise of organizing a game of ball. The remainder of the children were happily occupied, and for the first time Laura was able to turn her attention to her upper-class assistants. Leaving Giles and Maria Dalton in charge of the ballroom, she made her way to the small dining room, where food had been served to Lord and Lady Countisbury, Lord and Lady Monksleigh, and Dr. and Mrs. Norris. When the rector saw her come in, he immediately said, "Do sit down and have some refreshment, Lady Dartmouth. I will go and lend my assistance in the ballroom."

Laura smiled at him gratefully. "Thank you, Dr. Norris. Things are rather quiet at the moment. His lordship took the older boys out on the lawn to play ball, and the little ones are still eating. But I'm sure Sir Giles would be glad of a chance to sit down, if you'd care to relieve him."

"Certainly," said Dr. Norris, who was a very scholarly, very religious, and very nice man.

Laura accepted some food from one of her footmen and said serenely to her friends, "Mark is so wonderful with boys. It must come from all his years in the navy. He just seems to understand them."

There was absolute silence as her guests all exchanged glances over her unconscious head. "Er ... yes ... quite," said Lord Monksleigh finally.

Lady Monksleigh cleared her throat. "Laura," she said a little awkwardly, "has Lord Dartmouth spoken to you about your accident? About the phaeton, I mean?"

"The phaeton?" Laura looked around at the five faces seated at her table. "What do you mean, Louisa? The wheel came off the phaeton. That's how I was thrown."

There was another silence, and this time Laura registered its strangeness. She put down her fork. "What do you mean?" she asked Lady Monksleigh directly.

That lady hesitated and then looked at her husband. "The wheel shaft on the phaeton was sawed through, Lady Dartmouth," he said heavily. "I spoke to Dartmouth about it Thursday afternoon. I thought he would certainly have told you."

"Perhaps," said Lady Countisbury with deadly sweetness, "he fired one of the stableboys."

Laura felt her breath beginning to come shallowly. What were they talking about? What were they insinuating? She stared about her with pale cheeks and wide, frightened eyes. "Sawed through?" she said.

"Yes," came the voice of Lord Monksleigh. "Bertram saw it first and called my attention to it. There wasn't a doubt of its being deliberate, I'm afraid."

"But who?" said Laura dazedly; and then, as

they all looked down at their plates, she knew.
They thought Mark had done it. But good God—
why? Why should he do such a thing?

She pushed back her chair. "Excuse me," she
said. "I must get back to the children." And
fled.

14

Laura was deeply upset by Lord Monksleigh's revelation. She got through the rest of the day in a daze, her body going efficiently through the motions that had to be done while her mind was in a chaotic whirl. Her first impulse was to dismiss Lord Monksleigh's words; he was mistaken, she told herself. He had to be mistaken. There was no *reason* for anyone to want to harm her.

But Lord Monksleigh had said that Mr. Bertram had also seen what he had. The shaft had been tampered with. That was evidently a fact, and she must accept it as such.

But why? And who? And why had Mark not told her?

The children eventually departed, tired and happy, and she and Mark were left alone together. They went by mutual unspoken consent into the yellow saloon. Laura sat down in a comfortable chair and Mark went to stand by the chimneypiece. Now, she thought, now he will certainly say something. He must know that the Monksleighs would have told me about the wheel. "The party went very well, I thought," he said in a cool level voice.

"Yes," returned Laura. She folded her hands in her lap and sat very still, her eyes on her husband. He looked very tall as he leaned against the graceful marble chimneypiece.

"Dr. Norris appears to be a thoroughly decent man. He's new since I left. A distinct improvement over our former rector, I thought."

"Yes," she said again. "He is a very fine person, an excellent clergyman and scholar. We are fortunate to have him."

A silence fell and Laura thought to herself incredulously: He isn't going to mention it. She looked searchingly at his face and he returned her look calmly, his face without expression but for a light, watchful look in the eyes. For a long moment they looked at each other across an invisible barrier of apprehension and constraint. Then he pushed himself away from the wall and came across to where she was sitting. He held out a hand to her and she put her own in it, very conscious of his closeness, of the lean strength of his body as she rose to her feet and found herself beside him. For a brief second his hand tightened over hers, and then he released it. "Shall we go up to bed?" he asked.

"Yes." Her voice was a little uncertain, a little breathless. "I suppose we should." As they went up the stairs she could feel his hand, possessive and demanding, on the small of her back.

If Laura had had any doubts about the opinion of her friends and neighbors in regard to her accident, they were resolved the following morning. It was Easter and she and Mark and Robin went together to church. It was clear, from the moment they alighted from their carriage, that Mark was *persona non grata*. There were warm smiles for Laura and Robin, frosty nods for Mark. No one quite dared to cut him completely, but it was obvious everyone would have liked to. Laura's cheeks were very flushed as they walked up the center aisle to take their places in the family pew at the front of the church.

The Easter service was lovely, but Laura could not concentrate on it. She seemed to feel hundreds of eyes boring into the back of her head throughout the prayers, the hymns, and Dr. Norris' really excellent sermon. She glanced once or twice at Mark as Dr. Norris was speaking from the pulpit, and the loneliness of his taut, uplifted profile filled her with unexpected pity and tenderness. She couldn't bear to see that remote, guarded look come back to his face and felt a surge of anger against all the well-meaning people who had put it there. As the service ended and they went back down the aisle, she slipped her arm through her husband's and walked very close beside him, her other hand holding Robin's. Once they were outside, she said, "I'm not feeling very well. I'd like to go straight home, if you don't mind."

"Of course, Laura," said Mark very quietly. He handed her into their carriage and he and Robin climbed in afterward. Their ride home was silent except for Robin's innocent chatter.

The week following Easter was outwardly much like any of the weeks that had preceded it. Maria Dalton and Sir Giles Gregory visited Laura at different times, and both attempted to bring up the question of the damaged phaeton. To both, Laura said in a clipped, tightly controlled voice, "I am not going to discuss that topic. If you persist I will have to ask you to leave." Both her friends had obediently changed the subject, but their grave, concerned faces did nothing to sooth Laura's own perturbation.

There was nothing to do, she decided, but to take each day as it came. She tried to put the memory of Lord Monksleigh's words out of her mind. The phaeton wheel, she decided, had been sawed through by some malicious prankster. It had quite possibly been meant to harm Mark, not her. After all, it was Mark's phaeton. She simply could not, would not, believe that her husband wished to hurt her. It was impossible.

It took her the better part of the week before she realized that John Evans, the sailor whom Mark had rescued in London and employed, was following her. At first she had thought his unusually frequent presence was a coincidence. By Saturday, when she saw him waiting across the street as she came out of the library in Dartmouth, she was certain that coincidence played no part in his persistent appearances. He was following her. And he was utterly devoted to Mark and had been under her husband's direct orders ever since he had come to Castle Dartmouth.

*　　*　　*

The weather turned cold for a few days, then warm. Laura and Robin got out their fishing poles and took to going down to the lake which lay at the far end of the deer park. There were several delightful spots that one could fish from and there was also a small rowboat that Laura used occasionally. She had always refused to take Robin out in the boat. She could not swim and was always afraid that if he got excited for some reason and tipped them over, they would both drown. Consequently, she took the boat out only when he was not with her.

Robin liked to fish and was remarkably patient for a five-year-old, but he simply was not up to sitting still for hours while waiting for a bite. Laura was. There are those for whom fishing is a pleasant pastime and those for whom it is a passion; Laura belonged to the latter category.

The weather was not ideal for fishing, as it was unusually sunny, but Laura badly needed a distraction and for a solid week went down to the lake every day after Robin's lessons, returning at teatime with a few unimpressive-looking trout and a large appetite. Robin came with her twice, and both times teased her to put the boat into the water, but she would not. "Perhaps Papa will take you out one day," she told him placatingly. "He can swim."

"Papa's too busy," said Robin with unaccustomed sulkiness. And it was true. In the last weeks Mark had been spending even more hours than usual in the library.

"Well, we'll ask him," said Laura. "But you

are not coming out with me, Robin, so stop badgering me."

The Monksleigh ball was scheduled for the last week in April, and Laura was reluctant to attend. She asked Mark if he wanted to go, but he simply raised his brows and said coolly, "Why not?" Laura knew very well why not, but they had gotten to a point where the only real communication between them took place in bed. It was not a happy situation.

The day before the ball was cool and overcast, a perfect day for fishing. Laura left Robin in the charge of one of the maids and headed happily for the lake. She was distracted for about fifteen minutes by the unexpected arrival of Giles Gregory, who, after a brief conversation, decided to accompany her. As Giles had fished with her before and she knew she could trust him to be an undemanding companion, she obligingly provided him with a pole and the two set off together on foot. They walked slowly, chatting amiably, and arrived finally at the lake, planning to put the small boat into the water. Before they had come out of the trees they heard Robin shouting and both broke into a run, arriving on the shore to find that the boat was not in its accustomed mooring but out in the middle of the lake. Robin was in it.

"Robin, bring that boat back here this instant!" Laura shouted furiously.

"I can't, Laurie," the little boy screamed back. "I can't move it. It's all full of water!"

"Oh, my God." Laura turned to look at Giles. He was deathly white.

"I can't swim," he said in anguish.

"Oh, my God," Laura repeated. She waded a little way into the cold water, and Giles grabbed her arm. "He's out too far, Laura. You can't get to him. It's too deep."

Giles was right. The lake was shallow for the first ten feet and then dropped steeply after that. Robin was twenty yards from shore. "Robin!" called Laura, desperately trying to keep panic from showing in her voice. "Try to push with the oars."

"I can't!" he cried. He stood, tears running down his face, arms held out toward her. "Laurie, help me!" he screamed.

There was the sound of someone crashing through the trees, and then Evans was on the shore beside them. "Jesus Christ!" he said when he saw Robin and the sinking boat.

"Evans, thank God!" Laura grabbed his arm. "Can you swim?"

"No, my lady, I can't." The man's voice was as anguished as Giles's had been. "I'll run for his lordship."

"Laurie!" screamed Robin. The boat was far down in the water now.

"What's going on here?" said a deep, familiar voice, and Mark was beside them. He took one look and sat down on the grass. "Evans, help me with these boots," he said tersely. Evans dragged the boots off, and Mark stood up, shrugging out of his coat. He waded into the water. "I'm coming to get you, Robin," he called

127

reassuringly. "Just stay calm, son." He plunged in and began to swim strongly for the boat.

The group on shore watched with hammering hearts as the powerful strokes carried Mark closer and closer to the sinking boat. "Please, dear God, please . . ." Laura prayed, and for a brief second closed her eyes. When she opened them again, Mark was at the boat. Robin, standing waist-deep in water, grabbed at his father. There was a brief struggle in the water as it looked as if the frantic boy were going to drown both of them, and then Mark was swimming back toward the shore, Robin's head braced firmly on his shoulder. Laura waded into the lake up to her thighs and stretched out her arms; Mark put Robin, soaking wet and crying, into them. They stood for a minute in the cold water, the three of them close together, Laura murmuring over and over, "It's all right now, darling. You're safe. It's all right."

Then Mark said, "He's too heavy for you. Give him to me." He picked Robin up effortlessly and carried him out of the water.

Robin clung to him, saying over and over, "I'm sorry, Papa. I'm sorry."

"Yes, I know you are," Mark replied matter-of-factly. "Here, now, I'm going to put my coat around you. You're freezing." Robin was set down on his feet, and Mark wrapped his own russet coat around his small shivering son. He looked at Laura. "He's all right, but we'd better get him home."

Laura nodded. Her wet dress clung to her legs and she too was beginning to shiver. "We all need dry clothes and a hot drink," she said briskly. Mark bent, picked Robin up once more, and started back the way he had come. Laura walked close beside him, and Giles and Evans brought up the rear.

15

As soon as they arrived back at Castle Dartmouth, Mark prescribed brandy for himself, Laura, and Robin, all of whom were distinctly chilled. Then Laura put Robin in a hot tub. The combination of the shock, the spirits, and the tub was enough to make him very drowsy, and Laura suggested bed. In a very short time he was asleep and she went back to her own bedroom, where a similar tub was awaiting her.

She was sitting in front of her dressing table wearing a pale apricot-colored dressing gown and having her hair brushed when Mark came in. He had changed into dry clothes and looked reassuringly normal. "That will be all for the present," Laura said to her maid, and when the girl had gone, turned to look at her husband. "Thank God you were there," she said simply. "I thought he was going to drown in front of me." And then she began to cry helplessly, her hands to her face, the tears dripping out between her fingers.

There was a movement from Mark, and she expected to feel his arms around her, but nothing came. After a minute she looked up, the tears still streaming down her face, and saw that he had sat down in a satin padded chair. He was watching her steadily, a white look about his mouth.

"Laura," he said, "who is the person who always uses that boat?"

The question was quiet, but she sensed behind it some intolerable strain. "Why, I am," she said. Then her eyes widened as she realized what he was saying. "You don't mean . . ." Her voice broke off.

There was a silence. He said, not pleasantly, "I am merely pointing out to you what I am all too certain will be shortly called to your attention by others. In the normal course of events, it would have been you in that boat." She met his eyes. "When was the last time you had it out?" he asked.

"Two days ago," she answered out of a dry throat.

"And it was all right then? It wasn't taking on water?"

"No. No, it was dry." She was very white now, and there was a look of strain over her cheekbones, as if the skin was stretched too tightly. Her eyes looked very dark. "Mark . . ." she said uncertainly, "what are you saying?"

"Only what everyone else will say," he repeated. "The boat was tampered with."

"But who would do such a thing?" she whispered.

He rose to his feet and stood looking at her.

There was utter silence in the room. Her impulse was to throw herself into his arms, to beg for reassurance, but something held her rooted to her seat. "I don't know," he said at last. He sounded tired. "I shall try to find out." Without another word he turned and left the room.

Laura stayed where she was for quite some time after he had gone. Her knees and her hands were shaking. Was it true? Was someone actually trying to harm her? Perhaps to kill her? If she had taken that boat out today, as she most certainly would have done had Robin not decided to disobey orders, she would be dead by now. And Giles too, she thought with horror. He could not swim either. If Mark had not come along, Robin would have met the fate planned for her.

A strange sense of unreality swept over her as she sat there in her beautiful bedroom. Why had Mark been there? He hadn't been out of the library all week, yet just at the time the boat would normally have been launched, he had appeared.

She felt suddenly hot and clammy, and the room began to go out of focus. Abruptly she put her head down, and then, after a minute, stumbled over to the bed and lay down. She felt too unwell to go down to dinner that evening, and Mark did not stop by to see how she was.

They did not go to Lady Monksleigh's ball the following evening. Laura simply could not face the ordeal of pretending that nothing had happened. She was not sure that Giles would have reached the same conclusions about the accident as Mark, but she was certain that he would have told the tale of Robin's near-fatal prank to every one of their friends. She could not cope with the sympathy, the horror, or the suspicion. "I just cannot go," she told Mark in a tense voice, and he had said he would send a message with their regrets.

The day after the ball Lady Monksleigh called on her. Laura refused to see her. She refused to see Maria Dalton as well. Giles, taking advantage of his privileged position as Robin's uncle, got to her through the child. It was four days after the incident at the lake, and Laura was cutting flowers in the garden when Giles tracked her down. "I have to talk to you, Laura," he said determinedly. "You must face up to things, you know. You cannot keep hiding from the truth."

Laura laid down her basket and her scissors. "What truth, Giles?" she asked.

"The truth that you are in danger," he returned brutally. "Laura, please listen to me. You must leave Castle Dartmouth."

She stood with her head bowed, her eyes on the lovely flowers heaped in her basket. "No," she said.

"For God's sake, Laura"—Giles was almost shouting—"don't you realize what is going on here? That boat was tampered with! If Robin hadn't been naughty and taken it out, you would have. You would have drowned."

"No, I wouldn't," she replied stubbornly. "Mark

would have rescued me, just as he rescued Robin."

"Would he have, Laura?" Giles's voice was quiet now, almost ominously so. "I tend to doubt that."

"Giles"—there was a desperate note in Laura's voice—"don't say that! Mark has no *reason* to wish harm to me."

He put his hands up to his eyes and his voice was scarcely a thread of sound. "I wonder if he needs a reason."

"What do you mean?" she whispered in return.

There was a pause, and then he answered in a voice he was obviously striving to make normal. "Just that Mark seems to be an unlucky husband. Look"—he took her hands and held them tightly—"maybe I've got this all wrong, maybe he's as pure as the driven snow, but *something* is wrong here. You have had three nearly fatal 'accidents' in less than two months. For your own safety, for my peace of mind, will you *please* go visit your parents for a few weeks?"

He was holding her hands so tightly he hurt her. Gently she pulled away from his grip. "I'll think about it," was all she would say.

She did think about it. She had, unfortunately, a great deal of time to think in. She could not bring herself to go back to the lake. She would not visit any of her friends or go into town, where she might meet someone. She even stayed away from her usual visits to the orphanage. And she lay awake at night, tossing and turning, her mind filled with fears and doubts.

She saw Mark only at dinner; the rest of the time he worked. He was closeted in the library all day and returned to it immediately after dinner. They had reached the point she imagined he must have reached with Caroline. They inhabited the same house, and that was the extent of their relationship.

It was a situation Laura found intolerable, yet she did not know what to do about it. They spoke only in the presence of the servants. It was impossible for Laura to discuss the possibility of her going on a visit to her parents; it was impossible to discuss anything with him. She thought this as she sat watching him at dinner ten days after the incident at the lake. He was unaware of her gaze, occupied in looking down at his wineglass, his face remote and still. The light from the chandelier threw a dramatic shadow from his lowered lashes across the hard line of his cheek. He is so utterly shut in on himself and alone, she found herself thinking. I can't reach him. But what had caused his steady withdrawal, she did not know. Was it really possible he wanted to hurt her?

She lay in bed that night, sleepless as usual, and listened for Mark's step next door. It didn't come, and at two in the morning she got up, put on a warm velvet robe, took a candle, and made her way downstairs to the library. The image of his solitary figure at dinner that evening was preying on her mind. She was, she realized with a flash of slightly hysterical amusement, worried about him. But though she told herself she must be insane, that if she had any sense at all she would be avoiding him, not seeking him out, her steps did not falter as she walked down the huge open staircase and through the great hall to the library.

16

The door was closed, but a light showed underneath it, and slowly Laura pushed it open. Mark was sitting slumped behind his desk, which contained, instead of the usual meticulous charts, several wine bottles, all of them empty. At first Laura thought he was asleep, but as she stepped farther into the room his lashes' lifted suddenly and he looked at her. She felt her heart jolt once, and then she said with forced calm, "I came to see if you were all right. It is two in the morning."

"You came to see if I was all right." His voice was perhaps more precise than usual, but unslurred. "That's funny, Laura." He seemed to realize for the first time that he was seated and she was standing, and slowly and carefully he rose to his feet. He seemed perfectly normal; if it hadn't been for the empty bottles, she would never have suspected he had been drinking.

"Come up to bed, Mark," she said softly. "It's late."

His teeth showed for a minute, white against his hard mouth. "Is that an invitation?" he asked insolently.

Instinctively she put her hand behind her and felt the doorknob. "No," she said. "It is not."

He began to walk across the room toward her. She stood still, with her hand on the knob, her back against the door. Her retreat was only a step away, yet she couldn't for the life of her take it, any more than she could reach up with her other hand to push him away. "Laura . . ." he said. She could see, now that he was so close, that his eyes were heavy with wine.

She tried to speak, but nothing would come. Then he had her in his arms, and lowering his face to hers, began to kiss her. For a moment she was passive under the bruising power of his mouth, sensing something in his embrace that had never been there before. With a slight shock she recognized it as desperation. Later she was to think that if she had had any sense at all she would have pushed him away and run. She did neither. Instead, she put her arms around his neck and clung to him, answering his need with the yielding sweetness of her mouth and body.

When he finally let her go and spoke, she hardly recognized his voice. "You're right," he said, "it's time for bed." His voice might have been slurred and unsteady, but his steps were firm as he picked her up in his arms and carried her up the stairs to her bedroom.

*   *   *

When Laura awoke late the following morning, she was alone. She lay still for a while, remembering the passionate abandon of the night before, and thinking. What to do? What to do? Her instincts told her one thing, her reason something else. Did she feel as she did about Mark only because of a physical attraction? Was she so shallow that she was ready to ignore all the evidence against him just because she adored making love with him? Her feelings for him on that level really counted for nothing, she told herself. He was perfectly capable of deliberately setting out to bring her under his domination; she knew that. She had seen him exercise his power before. If only there were someone she could trust to talk to; someone who would be unshocked and discreet and sensible to help her see things as they really were.

It came to her as she rang for her maid to help her dress that in fact there *was* someone. She didn't know why she hadn't thought of him before. She would go talk to Dr. Norris.

She felt immediately better at the thought of doing something about her dilemma, and determined to go this afternoon, after she had given Robin his lesson. And since she had been having such a dangerous time with other conveyances lately, she decided to ride. There was a ripple of surprise when she appeared at the stables dressed in her riding habit, and even more surprise when she announced that she would personally saddle her mare. There were, however, no questions. The gossip about her accidents was not confined to the upper class of Dartmouth alone.

Laura carefully examined each piece of tack before she put it on the mare. The bridle was intact. The stirrup leathers on her saddle were in equally good condition and her girth was whole and soft and clean with saddle soap. She checked twice to see that it was tight enough before she finally mounted and rode out of the stable yard. There had been absolute silence the whole time she had been in the stable.

It was not until she was cantering along the path that Laura realized how confined she had been feeling, how good it was to be out and exercising again. It was perhaps a twenty-minute ride to the rectory, and Laura was received graciously by Mrs. Norris. The rector was not in at present, she told Laura regretfully. He had gone to visit several sick parishioners. Mrs. Norris expected him back shortly, however, and asked if Lady Dartmouth would care to wait.

Laura said she would, and sat down to have a pleasant cup of tea with the rector's wife. Mrs. Norris made absolutely no mention of Laura's accidents, but chatted calmly and amusingly about the doings of her children. Laura had always liked the rector's wife and now she found herself more and more impressed with the tact and the quite genuine goodness of the woman.

"You are fortunate to have such lovely children," she said sincerely. "I want very much to have children as well, but so far . . ."

Mrs. Norris looked at Laura's unhappy face

and smiled gently. "It was almost a year before I conceived Richard," she said comfortingly. "And now look—I have five. It doesn't always happen right away. I shouldn't worry about it if I were you, Lady Dartmouth."

Laura brightened. "A year?" she said.

"Yes. You haven't been married for nearly that long. And I should imagine things are rather . . . tense just at present. That doesn't help." It was the closest she came to mentioning the situation at Castle Dartmouth. After an hour, when the rector still had not come in, Laura took her leave. She had not accomplished her purpose, but she felt much better for her talk with his wife.

Laura took her favorite shortcut across the park on her way home. It was a lovely sunny day and the mare seemed as pleased as she to be galloping along on the spring-softened turf. They approached the ha-ha at a strong, steady gallop and the mare's ears flicked forward. Laura leaned forward over her neck, saying, "Now, my lovely." The mare took off with faultless precision; this was a jump she had made countless times before. They were in the air over the ditch when the world was shattered by a blinding shaft of light. Laura could see nothing. She felt the mare falling beneath her, and more from instinct than from reason she pushed herself out of the saddle. She hit the ground and knew no more.

When she awoke she was in her own bed. "She's coming round now," said a man's voice, and she opened her eyes to see Dr. Redding.

"There you are, my lady," he said encouragingly. "How do you feel?"

"My head hurts," she said faintly after a minute.

"I imagine it must," he replied sympathetically. "You took quite a nasty fall."

There was a movement behind the doctor, and Mark came into view. "What happened?" she asked him.

"We were hoping you could tell us," he answered in a tense voice. "You were jumping Annabel over the ha-ha when she fell."

"Yes." Laura remembered it now—the flash of light that had splintered the day. "Annabel?" she asked.

No one answered her at first, and she struggled to push herself up. "Lie still, Laura!" in Mark's sharp voice overrode the doctor's more temperate "Please don't disturb yourself, Lady Dartmouth."

Laura lay back, her head throbbing, and Mark said, "The mare broke her leg, Laura. I'm sorry." She looked at him and for a moment saw real anguish in his eyes. "Thank God you had the presence of mind to jump clear of her. If she had fallen on you, you might have been killed."

She closed her eyes. "That's a phrase I seem to be hearing a great deal of these days," she said.

The doctor coughed. "You most assuredly have a concussion, Lady Dartmouth. I want you to stay in bed for a few days."

"Yes, doctor," she said listlessly.

"I am leaving a sleeping draft for you. Rest is most important."

"Yes," said Laura again. "Thank you, doctor."

When she opened her eyes again, both Dr. Redding and Mark had gone.

She obeyed the doctor and spent the next few days in her room. At least there, she thought, she was safe. But she was not safe elsewhere; that was now perfectly plain.

Mark did not come to see her. It was from the housekeeper that she learned Evans had seen her fall and brought her back to the house. The ubiquitous Evans, she thought.

Why would anyone want her dead? The evidence all pointed to Mark, but he had no *reason* to wish ill of her. She had some money, but he had a great deal more. She simply could not believe, as Giles had suggested, that Mark would act without a motive.

The evidence, she thought. What was the evidence?

First, there was the incident at Dartmouth Castle. Mark had suggested that she go up to the North Tower, and he had called her from the courtyard so that she would almost certainly lean over the parapet to answer him. It had only been by the luck of her caught cloak that she had not fallen to her death. But then, she remembered also, Mark had rescued her. If he had wanted her dead, surely he would have left her there—or pushed her over when there was no one to see what he was about.

Then there was the phaeton, with the sabotaged wheel. Almost anyone had access to the carriage house. The damage did not have to be done by anyone from the estate.

There was the incident at the lake. The boat had been meant for her; she was dead certain of that. And Mark had been on the scene, which was unaccountable when one looked at his habitual routine.

And now the accident at the ha-ha. Someone had shone a mirror into the eyes of the mare, someone who must have been hiding among the trees, someone who knew she had gone out and who knew how she would be returning home.

The evidence stacked up neatly and made quite a damning case, she thought. And in the eyes of the world, Mark was already responsible for the death of another young woman. It was virtually impossible to refrain from holding him culpable.

It was while she was lying on her chaise longue watching Robin build with blocks that the answer came to her. The more she thought about it, the clearer it became. She thought of Mark's face, of how he had looked this last month, and bitter anger began to burn in her heart. Why hadn't she seen it before? she castigated herself. Of course there was a motive; she had just been too self-involved and frightened to see it.

17

It was not until three days after her accident that she saw Mark. She was in the nursery tucking Robin into bed when he came into the room. Together they bent over the child, and then, as he closed the nursery door behind him, Mark said quietly, "I must talk to you."

"Yes," said Laura. "I want to talk to you as well. Come down to my room."

They walked in silence down the stairs and along the corridor to Laura's bedroom. She was feeling tired and went to sit in one of the chairs in front of the fire, gesturing Mark to the other. He shook his head and stayed by the door, as if afraid to trust himself to come any closer.

"Someone shone a mirror into the mare's eyes," she said without preamble. "That's why she fell."

"I know," he replied in a colorless voice. "Evans found it among the trees." He put a hand up to his forehead for a minute and then said, "Laura, I want you to go away from Castle Dartmouth. Go to your parents or to Aunt Maria. You are well enough to travel now, so I suggest you leave tomorrow. You may take Robin with you."

"If I do that," she replied soberly, "everyone will most certainly blame you."

"What does it matter?" he said with weary bitterness. "They can't blame me any more than they do now, more than I do myself for keeping you here for as long as I have."

She looked at his shadowed face. "Mark," she said very softly, "darling, who hates you so much that he would try to destroy you like this?"

She had thought he was still before, but at her words he went, if possible, even stiller. "What do you mean?" he said.

"I mean that these accidents aren't really directed at me, are they? They are meant for you—to destroy your good name, your marriage, your career, perhaps even your sanity. Why, Mark? Why? And who?"

"God, Laura, I don't know!" The words were a cry of anguish. "I've racked my brain until I *did* think I was going insane, but I don't know! All I know is someone is using you to get at me. And I can't allow it to continue any longer. The next time, you might not be lucky. You must get away from here!"

"Only if you'll go with me," she said firmly, and stood up.

There was a pause; then his shoulders came away from the door in a kind of a lunge and he was across the room and had her tightly in his arms. He held on to her as a drowning man about to go down for the last time might hold onto a safety device that someone has thrown to him. Laura put her own arms about him, pressing herself against him, feeling the strong muscles of his back under her hands. They stood like that, locked together, for quite some time. Then, reluctantly, he loosened his hold a little and held her away so he could look into her face. "How did you know?" he asked shakily.

"I didn't know until yesterday," she answered honestly. "I was so confused ... and scared, too. Everything seemed to point to you, yet somehow I couldn't make myself believe that you were capable of murder. It just went against every instinct I had, to believe that of you. But it seemed as if I *had* to believe it. It wasn't until yesterday, when the thought crossed my mind that *you* were being as badly hurt by this business as I was, that the truth finally dawned on me."

He looked very gravely into her face. "Everyone else seemed to believe I was capable of murder." The bitterness was there again under the deep steady notes of his voice. "Why couldn't you?"

She flushed a little. "Everyone else isn't married to you. You have always been so ... so good to me." She bit her lip. "I'm putting this badly. I mean, the way you behaved to me on our wedding night ... well, a man like that just doesn't go around murdering people."

For the first time in weeks there was a glint of amusement in his eyes. "How did I behave to you on our wedding night?" he asked.

She looked at his shoulder. "You were so gentle, so understanding . . . I knew you hadn't married me for love, but you have always . . . I mean, you . . ." She glanced up at him and saw the amusement. "Oh, you know what I mean!"

"I think perhaps you had better explain it a little more," he said teasingly.

She ignored him. "And then, the accidents were so clumsy. If you wanted to get rid of me, you would have been much cleverer. Why, you're a scientist! You don't need to do stupid things like sawing through phaeton wheels so everyone would be sure to notice. Really, the more I thought about it, the clearer it became that the accidents were staged not to kill me but to throw suspicion on you." She put her cheek against his chest. "I'm only sorry it took me so long to see it. But you . . . went away, rather. If I could have talked to you about it, I would have understood sooner." She raised her head and looked up at him. "*Why* didn't you tell me, Mark?"

He looked over her head, his eyes concealed by half-lowered lashes. "I couldn't. There had been all that talk about Caroline—how I had driven her to her death—and now there were these strange accidents befalling you. How could I expect you to believe that I wasn't some deranged wife-slayer? Everyone else believed it of me fast enough. How could I expect you to trust me with your safety? I didn't have the *right* to ask that of you." His eyes left the fire and came down to focus on her uplifted face. "I was afraid you wouldn't believe me," he said slowly. "And that I just could not have borne."

Her mouth quivered a little. "Oh, darling," she murmured. "I think I knew all along that it was impossible for you to hurt anyone. It was like a nightmare, like something out of *Macbeth*, where all the world is turned upside down and 'nothing is but what is not.'"

His hands very gently cupped her face. "I should have known," he said shakily. "I should have known that you were not like anyone else in the world." Then his mouth came down on hers and he was kissing her with a passionate intensity that awoke an instant response in her. She rose up on tiptoe and clung to him tightly. "Who said I didn't marry you for love?" he murmured finally against her hair.

"You did." She released her grip a little so she could look at him. "You said our marriage was a 'solution,' that you needed a mother for Robin, that you needed more children because one wasn't enough to 'secure the succession.'" There was a half-reproachful, half-accusatory note in her voice as she quoted those last words.

He looked a little sheepish. "Did I really say that?"

"You did."

"Well, I was trying to sound practical, Laura. I wanted you to marry me, you see. I wanted it very badly. I didn't want to frighten you away."

"You almost did!" she said indignantly. "You sounded horrible!"

"I'm sorry, love." He gathered her close again and put his cheek against her hair. "When you walked into the library that first day, I thought that I had never seen anyone more lovely in my life. To think that *you* were this motherly

Mrs. Templeton Aunt Maria had written me about!"

She chuckled. "You surprised me, too. You had been represented as rather an ogre, as I'm sure you must realize."

"I know," he replied a little grimly. "When I left England four years ago, I was ... oh, hurt and bitter, I suppose. And guilt-ridden, too. I *did* feel responsible for what happened to Caroline, you see. We did not have a happy marriage, as I'm certain you have heard by now. I just wanted to get away.

"And then I came home and you were here. You were so serene, so lovely, so sweet—I began to think that with you I might really be able to live happily at Castle Dartmouth after all. For the first time since I was a boy it felt like a home to me. It wasn't just Robin I wanted you for. It was for myself as well."

"Why didn't you tell me that?" she asked wonderingly.

"I didn't think you wanted to hear it. You never gave any sign that you regarded me as anything more than Robin's father. I thought that since that was my trump card, I had better play it." She heard the smile in his voice. "It worked."

"So it did," she replied sedately—or as sedately as she could, considering she was locked in his arms. "So it was my motherly qualities you coveted," she went on in the same tone.

"Your motherly ... ?" The words were almost a growl, deep in his throat. "My feelings for you, my girl, aren't remotely filial."

"Oh, aren't they?" she teased, deliberately provoking him.

"No." He picked her up in his arms and carried her over to the bed, where he began to undress her efficiently. His brown eyes were narrow and blazing. "Not at all," he muttered, and reached up to tear open his own neckcloth. A wave of desire rippled through her and she held out her arms to him.

"I love you so, darling," she said. "I love you."

18

It wasn't until a good deal later that the Earl and Countess of Dartmouth got around to discussing their chief problem again. "You must go away," Mark said definitely. They were both in dressing gowns and eating a light supper in front of the fire in Laura's room. They had neither of them felt like dressing for dinner. "I can't keep you safe here. Even with Evans playing bodyguard, someone has managed to get at you."

Laura put down her chicken wing. "So that's why Evans has been following me around," she said wonderingly.

"Oh, you noticed him." Mark cocked an eyebrow at her. "Did you think he was one of my minions out to get you?"

"The possibility crossed my mind," she said smoothly. He grinned and she thought with amazement: We can even joke about it now.

He went on, "Still, the fact remains that you simply aren't safe. If I stick to you wherever you go, it will only be grist to the enemy's mill. He wants to involve me."

"Well, on at least one occasion you saved us from a fatality," she said soberly. "If you hadn't been at the lake . . ." She looked at him curiously. "Why *were* you there, Mark? You hadn't been out of the library in days."

He looked a little rueful. "I saw you going off with Giles Gregory from the library window," he confessed. "I just didn't like to see you spending so much time in his company."

"You don't think *Giles* . . ." she said incredulously.

"No, no, nothing like that," he assured her hastily. "I was jealous, I suppose. The fellow always seemed to be hanging about you." He rumpled his hair a little. "I don't like Giles," he confessed. "I'm afraid he reminds me too much of Caroline."

"Oh," she returned softly. "He looks very like her, I believe."

"Very much." Mark took a sip of wine and thoughtfully regarded its sparkling effervescence. "I'd like to tell you about Caroline," he said. "Perhaps it will explain a few things to you."

"I'd like that," she replied gravely.

"I've never told anyone," he went on, still not meeting her eyes. "It isn't a story that redounds to anyone's credit—but you have a right to hear it." At this point Laura thought she did too, and so she said nothing and let him continue. She thought, as well, that it would be good for him to unburden himself finally on a subject that had obviously been a cause for great agony and great blame.

"I was twenty years old when I married Caroline," he began. "She was eighteen. I met her at Cadbury House in August of 1814. I had come home from duty in the eastern Mediterranean in June and it looked as if my career in the navy was finished. My elder brother had died the previous December, you see, leaving me the heir." He frowned a little and his gaze moved from the champagne to the fire. "Robert's death had aged my father unbelievably," he went on slowly. "He had always been so proud of Robert—of his shooting, his horsemanship . . ." Here he flashed a quick smile at Laura. "Robert would have been more up to your standard in that department," he told her.

"You are quite up to my standard, darling, I assure you." She smiled at him a little mysteriously and his eyes glinted in response.

"Yes, well, Robert's death hit my father rather hard," he continued resolutely. "One of the results was that he became hipped on the idea of my marrying and having a son. I can tell you he was absolutely obsessed with the idea. He was afraid something would happen to me and then where would the Cheney line be?"

"Whereas he wouldn't have minded your demise so much if you left a son or two behind," Laura murmured.

He grinned. "That was the general idea." Then, quick to read the expression on her face, he added, "You mustn't blame him, love. As I said before, Robert's death had changed him.

And one can't blame him either for loving Robert more than me; after all, Robert had always lived at home. I was away at sea from the age of eleven."

"I think it's disgraceful," Laura said, "pushing children into the navy at so young an age."

"It has its drawbacks," he admitted, "but by and large I liked it. Now, will you stop interrupting and listen?"

She folded her hands in her lap. "Yes."

"Thank you. Well, as I was saying, I had been home two months, two months of listening to Papa going on about my duty to my line, when I received an invitation to Cadbury. The Season was just over in London and they had some people down for a house party. I went, saw Caroline, and suddenly the idea of marrying didn't seem so distasteful."

He poured himself a little more champagne and sipped it thoughtfully. "In retrospect, I really can't blame myself for being bowled over. I certainly wasn't alone; she had had a tremendously successful Season. Half the party at Cadbury was composed of men who wanted to marry her. You know how good-looking Giles is—well, Caroline had the same fair-skinned, fine-boned beauty, but on her it looked ethereal. She had these huge innocent blue eyes and was so small and delicate—they had dubbed her the 'fairy princess' in London.

"So, one look, and I fancied I was in love. Amazingly, she seemed to return the sentiment, and when I proposed a month later, she accepted. We were married in October." He poured himself another glass of champagne and downed it. "I discovered on our wedding night that she wasn't a virgin," he said tersely.

"Oh," Laura breathed.

"It wouldn't have been so bad, Laura, if she hadn't tried to deceive me!" he said passionately. "If she had told me before, I think I could have accepted it—I really do."

"Were *you* a virgin? Did you tell her about *your* past experiences?" Laura asked gently.

His jaw set. "It's not the same thing," he said.

Laura sighed. "No, I suppose not."

"Maybe it ought to be," he admitted, "but in our society it just isn't. A man expects his young bride to be a virgin; she does not expect the same of him." His mouth twisted a little. "I told you this story did not redound to anyone's credit."

She reached across the table and briefly touched his cheek. "It's all right, darling. I understand. And you are right—she *should* have told you."

"Well, she didn't," he replied bleakly. "She left me to find out for myself. She was hoping, I think, that I wouldn't notice. Well, of course I got all indignant and accused her and she cried and we had a thoroughly unpleasant scene. It was not," he said with masterly understatement, "an ideal way to begin a marriage."

"No," Laura murmured sympathetically, "I can see that."

"We had gone to Cheney Manor, the estate in Derby, for our honeymoon. We stayed for two very uncomfortable weeks. I behaved badly —I admit it. But she *looked* so damn innocent and guileless, Laura. I just couldn't forgive her for deceiving me, for trying to fool me. After the two weeks, we returned to Castle Dartmouth, and about six weeks later Caroline told me she was going to have a child."

"Oh, no." Now Laura's eyes were wide with horror. "You mean Robin . . ."

"Yes. I mean Robin. I had slept with her only that one time, on our wedding night. I was too angry and hurt to go near her again. So of course I asked her the obvious."

"Whose child was it?" Laura's voice was small and fearful.

"Yes." His voice was grim. "This time she was truthful. She didn't know." A small sound came from Laura, and she put her hands up to stifle it. A muscle flickered in his jaw, but he went remorselessly on. "That left me with a hell of a choice. Either I made a huge scandal, acted the betrayed husband, and dragged us all through the mud, or I kept quiet and accepted the child as mine." He revolved his champagne glass slowly in his long fingers. "Under the circumstances," he said quietly, "I really had no choice. I said nothing."

"Mark, who was . . . ?" She couldn't finish the question.

"Her lover? I don't know. She wouldn't tell me."

Laura closed her eyes. "Dear God . . ."

"Yes, it was not exactly enjoyable. And I didn't make it any better," he said honestly. "Having made up my mind to accept her as my wife, to accept her child as my own, I should have tried to forget the past. But I didn't."

"It was not an easy situation," she said softly.

"No. But I didn't even try. I thought, very well, she can have my name and my home, but I'm damned if she's going to have *me*. I was going to make her suffer, you see. I even started to see some girl in the town."

"You were only twenty."

"That was part of the problem," he admitted. "I was too young to handle it all. Poor Caroline. She had been counting on me, I think, and I let her down."

"Then Robin was born . . ." Laura prompted.

"Then Robin was born. God, how I hoped he'd look like me! But he didn't. He was the image of Caroline. I used to look and look at him, trying to find a resemblance to me—or to anyone else I knew. There was nothing, only this miniature Caroline.

"Then my father died. While he had been alive I had tried to keep up some pretense of normality, but after he died we behaved like what we were—two strangers who happened to inhabit the same house. I had no idea it was so impossible for Caroline." He put his elbows on the table and rested his forehead in his hands. "You can imagine how I felt when she killed herself." His voice was muffled. "I was greatly at fault, Laura. She had erred, but I was the more to blame. Then all those rumors started circulating . . ."

"I'm sorry for her, of course," Laura said, "but really, darling, you mustn't blame yourself so much. After all, I had a husband who ignored me quite as thoroughly, and I assure you I never even *thought* of taking my own life. And I didn't have a darling little baby to live for, either."

He lifted his head. "That's true. But you are a much stronger person than Caroline."

"From what you've told me, that shouldn't be difficult."

A little of the look of strain left his eyes. "I applied for a ship almost immediately. I had to get away. And the Admiralty offered me the Turkish survey. It was the answer to a prayer, and I jumped at it. I was away for four years and during that time I came to some terms with what had happened. Mainly I determined that I would not make the same mistake with Robin that I had with Caroline. In the eyes of the world I had accepted him as my son, and I knew I had to treat him as my son, not as some pariah who happened to wash up on my doorstep."

"You have been marvelous with him," she assured him.

"It was easier than I thought it would be," he confessed. "I was nervous of meeting him. All I could remember was this baby looking up at me out of Caroline's eyes. . . . But Robin was a little boy, a distinct person in his own right. And a very likable person. It wasn't difficult at all." He smiled at her. "And then, you were there."

She didn't return his smile. "Robin may not have your coloring, but he *does* have a look of you, darling. And too, he is so tall . . ."

"No, Laura." His voice was quiet but firm. "That kind of speculation is exactly what I promised myself I would not do. Robin is himself and he deserves to be loved as himself. Whether he is mine by blood is not important. He is mine in every other way. My son. We must —neither of us—engage in fruitless and destructive guessing games about his parentage."

"Oh, Mark." She came around the table and knelt before him, her arms around his waist, her face against his shoulder.

He rubbed his chin against her hair. "It's not such an unusual decision," he said lightly. "You have loved him like a mother for years, and you have no blood ties to him."

"It's different for a woman," she murmured into his shoulder.

"I don't see why it should be."

She laughed a little and raised her head. There were tears in her eyes. "It's like virginity: there shouldn't be a difference, but there is." She put up a hand to smooth his hair back from his forehead. "If Caroline had only had some courage and patience, you would have come around to accepting her as well. You would have done it sooner, I expect, if she hadn't complicated matters by having a baby." She heaved a sigh and looked wistful. "How I should love to have a baby," she said longingly.

"Are you giving me a hint?" he demanded.

"Why, no," she murmured, startled and drawing back in his embrace.

He shook his head. "I can see you are. Well, love"—he stood up, drawing her to her feet—"if you're quite finished eating . . . ?"

"I am. You're not." She pointed to a piece of chicken left on his plate.

"I'm hungry for other things," he said, marching her toward the bed.

"I'm tired," she protested.

"Too bad. You said you wanted a baby. Well, let me tell you, making babies takes time. And effort." He pushed her back on the bed and then threw himself down beside her, one leg across hers, his face very close. "Are you prepared to cooperate?" he asked with mock severity.

A smile indented the corner of her lips, and her eyes were even smokier than usual. "Oh, well," she said, "if it's in a good cause."

"The best of causes, my love," he murmured, brushing his mouth against hers. "The very best."

III

. . . a generous and constant passion in an agreeable lover, where there is not too great a disparity in other circumstances, is the greatest happiness that can befall the person beloved.
—Richard Steele, *The Tatler*

19

Laura held firm about not leaving Castle Dartmouth unless Mark came with her. "I absolutely refuse to leave you here to face all the vicious gossip," she said steadily. "If you wish me to go, we will have to go together."

"All right, Laura, all right," he had finally given in. "God, but you're stubborn."

"Only when provoked," she returned sweetly.

There was silence as she stirred her coffee. They were sitting in Laura's private sitting room having breakfast. "Where will we go?" she asked at length.

"I think perhaps to Cheney Manor in Derbyshire," he answered slowly. "It's a nice little manor house and it shouldn't take too long to get it ready for us. There is a caretaker couple living in the house and no other servants aside from a few gardeners to look after the property."

"Do you want to bring some servants from Castle Dartmouth?" she asked carefully.

"No, I do not. I don't want anyone near us

who has had access to you here." She nodded slowly and sipped her coffee. "We'll engage some servants from the area," he continued. "They may not be highly trained, but they'll be safe. I'll have Farnsworth get on it." He pushed his coffee cup aside. "In the meanwhile, Laura, I don't want you to set foot out of this house."

She sighed unhappily. "It makes me feel so wretched, Mark, suspecting everyone who comes near me. It's a horrible way to live."

"I know, and we'll remove to Cheney Manor as soon as possible. But until we do, I want you to stay in the house." He sounded very much like a captain giving orders to a subordinate; he wasn't asking, he was commanding.

"All right," said Laura. "It will be dreadfully tedious, but I'll stay in the house."

He rewarded her with a brief smile. "Good girl. Now, let me go and talk to Farnsworth."

It was ten days before they finally did arrive at Cheney Manor in Derbyshire. Mr. Farnsworth had had the house opened up for them and had engaged a minimal staff to assist the caretakers. The early-May weather was lovely, so Mark, Robin, and Laura drove in the phaeton, followed by two coaches loaded with their luggage. The only other horse they brought besides the carriage horses was Robin's pony.

Cheney Manor was a lovely old house built of mellow pink brick and set in a small but gracious park. It was not at all on the scale of Castle Dartmouth, but it was clearly the home of a gentleman. It had been in the Cheney family for several generations. Laura liked it immediately, and she liked as well the pleasant-faced couple who were to be the mainstays of her staff.

They arrived late in the day, and by the time Robin had seen his pony safely stabled, a task he insisted on doing himself, he was ready to drop with tiredness. Laura gave him his dinner in the large bright nursery on the third floor and tucked him into bed. He was asleep almost immediately.

She went down to her bedroom, where a pretty young girl was waiting to help her change her dress. Even Laura's personal maid and Mark's valet had been left behind at Castle Dartmouth. She put on a primrose-colored silk evening gown and went downstairs to join Mark at dinner. She felt freer and lighter of heart than she had in quite some time.

As her first week at Cheney Manor drew to a close, Laura's contentment had only deepened. The house was comfortable, and the staff, if inexperienced, was willing and pleasant. Mark had set up his charts in the library and was looking less strained with every passing hour. There were only two immediate problems that disturbed Laura's comfort: she needed a horse to ride, and Robin needed a friend to play with.

Careful inquiry had led her to believe that both of her problems might be solved in one place. The great house of the neighborhood was Wymondham, which belonged to David Wrexham, the Earl of Wymondham. From what Laura had discovered, the Earl had a huge stable of horses—mostly racehorses that he trained himself. And he also had four children, one of whom was about Robin's age.

Neither the Earl nor the Countess had called on the Dartmouths, a fact that Laura mentioned to one of the visitors who did call to welcome her to the neighborhood. "Lady Wymondham never calls on anyone," Lady Spenser told her with distinct asperity. "Really, as far as neighborhood social life is concerned, Wymondham is a dead loss. All she does is paint and hunt. *He* is much more pleasant"—and here Lady Spenser's face took on a look Laura recognized. She had seen it on women's faces when they looked at Mark. "But with a wife who is a veritable hermit, what can he do?"

This was rather daunting information, and Laura shared it with Mark. He surprised her by saying he had known the late Earl, Lord Wymondham's father. "I met him when I was out in Turkey," he told her. "He was a very impressive man, very interested in our survey, and even more interested in the archaeological finds we were making. He died not long after I met him—caught a bad case of fever. It was a damn shame, because he was a fairly young man."

"Why didn't you tell me you knew Lord Wymondham's father?" Laura asked indignantly.

"You never asked," he returned reasonably.

"Men are impossible," his wife announced, surveying him from head to foot. "Well, my lord, tomorrow you can just tear yourself away from your charts and accompany me to Wymondham. Your knowing the late Earl will be a good excuse to call."

"Not tomorrow," he said instantly. "I've almost finished this one particular chart of Rhodes, and I don't want to leave it."

"All right," she agreed. "Next day?"

He sighed. "Next day," he said. "I promise."

As it happened, Laura did not have to wait that long to meet at least three members of the Wymondham family. She and Robin went fishing the next day, and as they came out by the river, which separated Cheney Manor from the Wymondham estate, she saw a man and two boys fishing on the opposite side. The man had his back to her, and for a moment of shocked surprise she thought the tall figure was Mark. Then the man turned and she saw it was not. "Hullo," called the younger of the boys. "You must be the new people at Cheney Manor."

"Yes," called back Robin. "We are."

"Come on over and fish our side," the older boy invited Robin. "It's better over here." Robin flashed Laura a look, and she nodded at him.

"There's a bridge a short way down the river," called the man.

"Thank you," Laura returned, and she and Robin set off to cross over and come back up the other side. As they approached the Earl of Wymondham, for it must be he, Laura thought, she scanned him appraisingly and understood instantly the look on Lady Spenser's face. He was as tall as Mark and his coloring was similar. And he was, unquestionably, the most beautiful man she had ever beheld in her life. He smiled as she approached. "You must be Lady Dartmouth," he said in a deep, soft voice. "I'm Wymondham."

Laura held out her hand. "How do you do, my lord. I'm delighted to meet you."

"I say, I saw you cantering your pony in the north paddock the other day," the older boy said to Robin. "She's smashing."

Robin's whole face lit up. The boys were introduced as Philip, aged ten, and Richard, aged seven, and by the end of the morning the three children were wet, dirty, and thoroughly pleased with one another. Lord Wymondham, who was extremely nice, chatted idly to Laura, and when he learned she had not brought a horse with her, offered to let her ride one of his. "Come over tomorrow morning and have a look around," he invited her casually. "Wear a riding skirt and bring Robin. We'll see what we can do for you."

"Is Lady Dartmouth going to ride one of our horses, Papa?" Philip asked mischievously.

"Yes, if we can find something to suit her," he answered pleasantly.

"Wait till Mama hears," said Philip, and his greenish eyes sparkled with pleasurable anticipation.

Laura was delighted to be going to Wymondham, but she found herself distinctly nervous at the thought of meeting the Countess. Obviously Lady Wymondham was not as friendly as were her husband and children.

20

Laura dressed in her best riding habit the next day, a beautifully cut bottle-green outfit that she had bought in London the week before she was married and had seldom worn. She excused Mark from going with her—he was obviously dying to get back to his charts—and took Robin along in the phaeton. She drew up to the great front door of Wymondham, an impressive stone house set in a stunningly beautiful park, and was directed down to the stables by the butler, who ran down the stairs almost as soon as she pulled up.

The stables at Wymondham were a revelation. There were two huge blocks of barns and acres of enclosed grassy paddocks. The whole area had the busy hum of serious endeavor. A groom came to hold her horses and inform her that Lord and Lady Wymondham were in one of the stalls with an injured horse and would be with her in a moment.

"Hullo, Robin!" came a shout, and Richard

came into sight from inside one of the stable blocks. He came jogging over to them and asked eagerly, "Would you like to see my pony?"

"Yes!" answered Robin just as eagerly, and looked at Laura. "May I, Laurie?"

"You can come too, Lady Dartmouth," the boy said politely.

"Thank you, Richard, but I had better wait for your mother and father."

Richard cast a speculative look at Laura's faultlessly clad figure. "Hmn," he said cryptically through his nose. "I'll tell them you're here," he added with conscious courtesy.

Laura was beginning to thank him again when he interrupted, "Here they are now, Lady Dartmouth." Laura turned her head and saw the tall figure of Lord Wymondham walking toward her across the stableyard. He was accompanied by a small black-haired girl who held her head with unconscious arrogance. But surely this can't be the mother of Philip, Laura thought in amazement. Why, she can't be any older than I am.

They had reached her side, and Lord Wymondham smiled. "We're delighted you could come, Lady Dartmouth," he said with gentle courtesy. "May I introduce my wife?" He looked down at the black head near his shoulder. "Jane, this is Lady Dartmouth and her son, Robin."

"How do you do," said Jane Wrexham in a cool, crisp voice. She shook hands first with Laura and then, to his delight, with Robin. "The boys had a splendid time fishing with you yesterday," she told him. "Is Dickon going to show you the ponies?"

"Yes, I am, Mama," her son replied. "Let's go, Robin." The two boys went off together in perfect harmony.

"I'm so delighted that Robin has found some children to play with," Laura said with a smile. "He has been rather lonesome."

"Yes, they do need a friend," replied the Countess. "Luckily my boys have each other. We haven't sent Philip to school; he is studying with our rector. But another companion is always a welcome addition." She surveyed Laura critically out of extraordinary blue-green eyes. "David tells me you need a horse," she said. She had not yet smiled. "Why didn't you bring your own?"

There was something in the tone of the Countess's voice that was setting up Laura's back. "I had an accident with my mare a few weeks before we moved, and I never got around to replacing her."

"Oh," said Lady Wymondham. She looked even more skeptical than she had before.

"Most of our horses are racehorses and not hacks," put in Lord Wymondham calmly, "but I'm sure we can find something for you to use until you get your own."

"Yes," said Lady Wymondham. "There is always Star."

There was a flash of amusement in Lord Wymondham's eyes. "We might do better than Star, Jane," he murmured.

"I don't know," his wife replied. She looked Laura up and down, taking in the immaculate state of her habit. Lady Wymondham herself was wearing a shirt with rolled-up sleeves and what looked to be a divided skirt of ancient origin. "How well do you ride?" she asked Laura bluntly.

Laura's back was straight as a ramrod. "Very well," she answered crisply.

"Well, let's go out to the paddock," said Lord Wymondham. "We'll see how you do on Cassandra."

Lady Wymondham glanced quickly up at her husband but did not protest. The three of them proceeded to go to the first paddock, and the mare was brought. Laura automatically checked the girth and then allowed herself to be helped into the sidesaddle. She walked the mare around the paddock a few times and then moved into a trot. From the trot they went into an effortless canter. The mare's paces were beautiful, her mouth like silk. After a few turns Laura pulled up before the Wymondhams, who were leaning against the gate watching her. "She's just lovely," she said, patting the mare's glossy chestnut neck. With a start she realized that Lady Wymondham was smiling at her. "It was your habit that put me off," she said. "It looks so new. I do beg your pardon."

Laura found herself smiling back. "So I'm not to be given Star?"

"Star? For a rider like you?" Lady Wymondham looked horrified. "He's good only for children."

Lord Wymondham looked amused. "Jane doesn't mean to be insulting," he said, putting a brief hand on the nape of his wife's neck. "She's just rather brutally honest."

"I wasn't being insulting," she replied indignantly. "I was giving Lady Dartmouth a compliment." She looked back at Laura. "Do you hunt?"

"I adore to hunt."

"How perfectly splendid," said Lady Wymondham with a flashing smile. "Come on up to the house with me while I feed the baby, and then we can take a ride together if you like. The boys will give Robin one of their ponies."

"I should love that," said Laura sincerely.

Laura and Mark remained at Cheney Manor for the rest of May and all of June, and during that time Laura had no accidents. For the first time in months she and Mark were able to live a normal life. But always there, nagging at the back of her mind, was the unanswered question: Who?

She and Mark discussed it until they were sick of the subject, but neither of them came up with any answers. It was a mystery that put a tiny rent in the fabric of their happiness, but it could not rip it apart. They were too much in love to be really disturbed.

Mark had lost a good deal of the fine-drawn look he had acquired during the months of their ordeal. The atmosphere at Cheney Manor was peaceful; there was none of the tenseness and suspicion that had haunted him at Castle Dartmouth. The friendship of David Wymondham was also very good for him, Laura thought to herself one night as they were sitting in the drawing room after dinner playing chess. David was so calm, so even-tempered, so patient and gentle. It was impossible to be anything but relaxed in his company. She looked at the top of Mark's head as he bent over the board. The top of his hair had bleached out again in the sun. He had taken to riding out with the Wymondham racing string in the morning, and the exercise had been good for him. Jane and David had proved surprisingly tolerant of Mark's mediocre horsemanship. The Wymondhams, in fact, were rather in awe of Mark's intelligence and accepted in him lapses they wouldn't have dreamed of condoning in anyone less superior. If only, Laura thought to herself with something like anguish, if only we *knew*.

Toward the end of June, when matters still lay unresolved, Laura did something she wouldn't have dreamed of doing a month ago. She told Jane about her accidents.

The two women had taken the children—four Wrexhams and Robin—on a picnic down to the river. The three boys were fishing, Jane's four-year-old daughter, Mary, was happily lying on her stomach building a house with sticks she had collected, and eight-month-old Matthew was asleep on the blanket. "I never asked you, Laura," Jane said, "but why did you and Mark come to live at Cheney Manor? David says Castle Dartmouth is famous for its beauty."

Laura hesitated, looked into Jane's beautiful proud face, and told her. When she finished, Jane pulled her knees up, rested her chin on them, and stared at Laura wonderingly. "Do you know," she asked, "the same kind of thing once happened to us?"

"What!" said Laura, astonished.

"Yes. I've never told a soul, but David's cousin once made several tries at killing him. It was while David was still living at Heathfield, before his father found him." The story of David's lost-heir upbringing was familiar to Laura by now. "David's cousin Julian came to Heathfield on a visit—he wanted to marry me, can you believe it?" Jane looked scornful, and Laura smiled. "Well, Julian took one look at David, who is very like his father, and realized who he must be. Julian, you must know, was next in line for the title and the money—*if* Lord Wymondham's only son remained lost. So he tried to kill David by arranging 'accidents.'"

Laura shivered. "How did you stop him?"

"At first, like you, we had no idea who it was who was attacking David. When he wasn't successful, he had to come out into the open. He and David got into a fight and Julian fell off a cliff. It was a very satisfactory conclusion to our problem."

"Yes, I can see that," Laura replied a little dryly. "But, Jane, we have no idea *who* this is. He has not come out into the open, you see."

"That's because it isn't necessary for him to really kill you," Jane said calmly. "He only wants to make life hell for Mark."

"Yes, but *why*?" Laura almost wailed.

"Mark has done something to him, obviously. He has taken something this saboteur wanted, I should think. Has Mark evicted any tenants or anything like that?"

"Of course not," Laura said indignantly.

There was silence while Jane thought, her

brow puckered. "Do you know, Laura," she said slowly, "I shouldn't be surprised if this goes back to Caroline's death."

Laura stared at her, an arrested expression on her face. "What do you mean?"

"You said there were ugly rumors going round then too. That's odd, you know. One would think one's reaction to a man whose wife had killed herself would be sympathy. It sounds as if your saboteur was at work even then."

"I never thought of that," Laura said slowly.

"Was Caroline having an affair with someone else?" Jane asked bluntly.

Light blue-green eyes met Laura's dark smoky gaze. There was a pause. "I don't think it was an affair," Laura said, "but she was in love with someone else before they married."

Jane looked grimly triumphant. "I should look there," she advised. "Someone blames Mark for her death and is out to make him pay."

21

Laura shared Jane's thoughts with Mark, and though, upon reflection, he was inclined to agree that she might be right, they were still no closer to a solution to the mystery. "I have no idea who Caroline's lover was," he told Laura again. "And I think we're safe in assuming it was all over after we married. Men did not call on Caroline when she lived at Castle Dartmouth. If someone had, I would have heard about it from my father. He was confined to the house, and nothing escaped him."

"Perhaps when we go up to London we might hear something," Laura murmured.

Mark looked bleak. "God, Laura, I wish I hadn't got to go to London." The King was to be formally crowned as George IV on July 19, and Mark, as one of the peers of the realm, had been summoned to attend. His head lifted suddenly, an arrested expression on his face. "Just one moment. What do you mean, when 'we' go up to London? You are staying right here where you'll be safe."

Laura put down her hairbrush and turned to look at him. It was eleven o'clock at night and they were both in her room, Laura at her dressing table and Mark lounging in a comfortable chintz-covered chair. "I am not staying here," she said calmly. "I'm coming with you."

"No." His face took on what Laura had christened its "captain's look." "I won't permit it."

"Listen, darling"—she got up and went over to sit on his lap—"don't you see what a perfect opportunity the coronation gives us for showing our solidarity to the world? If the saboteur"— Laura had adopted Jane's phraseology—"sees that I am going to stick with you no matter what, he may simply give up trying."

"Or he may decide to really make an effort and kill you. No, Laura. We can't take the chance."

"*I* am willing to chance it."

"Well, I'm not." She was sitting upright on his lap and now he pulled her down so her cheek was against his shoulder. "You're the most precious thing I've got," he murmured into her hair. "I'm not risking *you*."

"It wouldn't be a risk, Mark," she argued into his shoulder, feeling at a distinct disadvantage in her present position.

"Yes, it would."

"No, only listen!" She pushed against his chest and sat up again. "I talked it all over with Jane this afternoon. She and David have to go to the coronation as well, and she's invited us to stay with them at Hawkhurst House, their town residence. It's outside London, in its own park on the Thames, so I should be quite safe there surrounded by the Wymondham servants. And when I go out, Jane has promised she will stick to me like a plaster. And we'll use only their carriages and horses." Laura paused, a little breathless from her rush of words. "Oh, darling, do say yes."

He looked gravely for a long minute into her eyes. Then he smiled a little and touched her cheek with the tip of his finger. "Laura ..." he began very gently, and she knew he was going to refuse.

"And there is another reason I should like to go to London, quite apart from this business of our saboteur," she added hastily.

"What is that?"

"I should like to consult Dr. Danbury." She leaned a little forward and gently kissed him on the mouth. "I'm going to have a baby, Mark."

"A baby ..." He looked suddenly very alarmed. "Are you all right? Why do you want to see a London doctor?"

Laura was feeling perfectly splendid, but she bit her lip a little and said too heartily, "Oh, I'm just fine, darling. But this man is very well-known, and I thought ..." She allowed her voice to trail off artistically.

"Of course you must see this Danbury," Mark said instantly. "Why didn't you tell me you weren't feeling well?"

Laura leaned against him and closed her eyes. She felt quite guilty about alarming him like this, but it was his own fault for being so stubborn, she thought defiantly. He held her close and she whispered, "Aren't you pleased about the baby?"

"I am because I know how much you want one. But if it's going to make you ill, I won't be pleased at all." His lips touched the silky skin of her temple. "Will you promise me not to stir from Jane's side?" His voice sounded tense.

She put her arms around his neck. "I promise."

He sat holding her quietly for what seemed a very long time. "You ought to go to bed, love," he said at last. "It's important for you to get enough rest."

"Mm," she murmured. "Come with me?"

"Are you feeling well enough?" His voice was so husky, so deeply tender. She trembled a little and thought she would really regret her deception about her health if he was afraid to make love to her.

"I told you I'm fine. It's . . . it's in the morning that I feel sick."

"In the morning. Well, isn't that convenient," he said, and now there was a thread of amusement in his voice. He stood up with her in his arms and began walking across the room.

"Convenient for whom?" she asked.

"For me," he answered, and laid her on the bed.

The Wymondhams came to Cheney Manor for dinner the following day, and over the meal the four of them discussed their proposed London visit.

"I can't tell you how much I appreciate your invitation," Mark told Jane. "I would not trust Laura's safety at Cheney House."

"I'll be delighted to have her company," Jane replied. "I hate London. Every fool in the world congregates there. But Hawkhurst House is nice. There are some splendid pictures."

"I haven't spent as much time in London in my whole life as I have this year," David grumbled. "I was stuck there from August through November at that ridiculous trial of the Queen's."

"He missed some of the hunting season," Jane put in. "Imagine!"

Mark grinned. "It boggles the mind," he said.

David chuckled. "Every other day I would get an indignant note from Jane. 'When are you coming home? The master told me they had a perfectly splendid run yesterday. Why don't you tell Prinny to take care of his wife by himself?' "

"Well, it was bad enough *I* wasn't hunting," Jane said. "I was expecting Matthew in December. Poor Mr. Denton was wretched. He's the master," she explained as an afterthought.

"Without the Wymondhams, the whole hunt falls apart, you see," David said gravely.

Jane shot him a look and snorted eloquently. Both David and Mark laughed.

"I must say, I'm glad I missed that show of Prinny's," Mark said sympathetically to David. "It must have been a regular horror."

"It was. All one could do was try not to listen. Of course she wasn't innocent, but, my God, Prinny's reputation is hardly saintly. It was all extremely distasteful. If Jane hadn't been enceinte, we would have left the country and gone to Italy for a few months."

Dinner came to an end and the two ladies

correctly withdrew, leaving the gentlemen to their port. Even before the door closed behind them, they could hear the two male voices in easy conversation. Mark and David really weren't alike at all, Laura reflected as she and Jane went into the drawing room, yet they had become very good friends. "They'll be there forever," Jane said, unconsciously echoing Laura's thought. "David adores talking to Mark. He says it makes him think."

Laura smiled and sat down across from her friend. It was impossible to believe that Jane was twenty-eight and had four children, she thought as she regarded the lovely face across from her. And speaking of children ... "I'm going to have a baby," Laura said. "Isn't that marvelous?"

Jane didn't look at all surprised. In her experience babies tended to come along with monotonous regularity. "Oh, dear," she said. "You won't be able to hunt this winter."

There was a stunned silence, and then Laura began to laugh. Jane regarded her in genuine puzzlement. "What is so funny?"

"You are," Laura told her. "As far as you're concerned, the entire world revolves around the hunting season."

Jane flashed a smile. "I suppose I do sound like that sometimes."

"Sometimes?"

"Well, I actually don't mind being enceinte and missing the hunting season once in a while," Jane confessed. "It gives me more time to paint. And when I consider that I've missed only four seasons in eleven years of marriage, I suppose I can't complain." She leaned forward and spoke very seriously. "The secret, Laura, is to nurse your children for as long as possible. It's the best way to ensure you don't become enceinte again too quickly. I've always nursed mine until they were enormous."

"But doesn't that bring on another problem?" Laura asked. "I mean, doesn't David object?"

"Object? Why on earth should he object? The children positively thrive."

Laura flushed a little. "I don't mean that. I mean, it's an awfully long time not to make love."

Jane looked astonished. "Not to make love? I didn't mean you didn't conceive because your husband didn't come near you. It's something to do with the milk, I think."

Laura frowned. "But I have always heard that a nursing mother should refrain from sexual relations. It is supposed to spoil the milk."

Jane gave her a scornful look. "I heard that story too. All I can say is, it never spoiled *my* milk. Well, I mean you only have to look at my children to see how healthy they are. Good heavens, I can just imagine David's face if I told him ..." She broke off and grinned. "I should have done it," she said. "It would have been hilarious."

Laura was staring at her in wonder. "Then you mean you never worried about it?"

"Of course not. I didn't believe it in the first place, but even if I did, the children are just splendid and I love them dearly, but David comes first."

Laura smiled radiantly. "Jane, you have just made me feel so much better."

"Yes," said Jane complacently, "it is always helpful to have an older friend to advise one."

There was the sound of male voices in the hallway, and then their husbands came into the room. For the remainder of the evening they continued the discussion about their upcoming London visit. Laura said she wanted to meet a few fashionable people who had known Caroline; she thought perhaps she might get a hint of who her previous suitors had been before she married Mark. "The problem is," she said ruefully, "I don't know any fashionable people."

"I don't either," said Jane. "But there is always Anne—my aunt. Or at least she is married to my uncle. It's silly to think of Anne as an aunt; she's only a few years older than I am."

"That's a good thought," David said approvingly. "The Marquis will have to be in town for the coronation the same as we."

"They're in London now," Jane said. "It's the stupid Season."

"And there is always Aunt Maria," Mark said reluctantly. "She is in town now as well."

"There," said Jane triumphantly. "We should be able to scratch up a few fashionable parties for you, Laura."

"Jane . . ." Mark's voice was quiet, but everyone looked at him instantly. "I am counting on you to stay close to Laura. Unfortunately, the way things are, she's safer if I keep away from her." He looked very tense about the nostrils.

"I promise you solemnly, Mark, she won't stir a step without me." Jane's eyes glittered with a tigerish ferocity, and Mark's face relaxed a little.

"I'm counting on you," was all he said in reply, and a few minutes later the Wymondhams took their leave.

A DOUBLE DECEPTION

22

The two couples arrived in London the first week in July. The only child to accompany them was Matthew; the others had all been left at Wymondham, with Robin feeling very grown-up and important to be going on a visit to his friends'. Hawkhurst House was, as Jane had promised, extremely beautiful. It made Laura homesick for her own beautiful home, and more than ever determined to get to the bottom of the mystery so they *could* return to Castle Dartmouth in safety.

Not long after they arrived, Jane sent a note around to the Marchioness of Rayleigh, her uncle's wife, and the following morning the Marchioness called. Laura tactfully withdrew upstairs and it was over an hour later that a footman sought her out to ask if she would join Lady Wymondham in the gallery. As Laura walked into the long, beautifully paneled room, she saw that the Marchioness was still there.

"Anne, this is Laura Dartmouth, whom I have

been telling you about," Jane said. "Anne is Lady Rayleigh, my uncle's wife," she explained to Laura.

"How do you do, Lady Rayleigh," Laura said with composure, and thought that the fair-haired, blue-eyed young woman most certainly did not look old enough to be Jane's aunt.

The Marchioness smiled. "Jane has been telling me of your dilemma, Lady Dartmouth."

Laura looked alarmed and cast a reproachful look in the direction of Jane's black head. Jane met her eyes straightly. "The story of your accidents is all over London," she said tersely.

"Oh, no!"

It was a cry of pure distress, and Lady Rayleigh answered in her gentle voice, "I'm afraid it is true, Lady Dartmouth. That is why I was so surprised when Jane told me you and Lord Dartmouth were here at Hawkhurst House."

"But how did the rumors start?" Laura asked.

"Who knows how these stories get around?" Anne replied.

"What exactly is being said?" Laura was rigidly upright on her chair, her hands clasped tensely in her lap.

"That you have been the victim of several attempts on your life," Anne replied bluntly. "Everyone recalls Lord Dartmouth's first wife, as well, and comments upon how chancy being married to him appears to be. There is some speculation as to whether she *really* committed suicide."

Laura went so white that Jane jumped up in alarm. Laura shook her head and forced a smile.

"I'm all right, really." She turned to Anne. "It's true enough that someone has tried to hurt me, but the real object of the attacks is my husband."

"Yes," said Anne, "so Jane has told me."

"Do you believe her?" Laura asked directly.

Anne looked for a minute at Laura's beautiful, pure face. "Yes," she said. "I do." She smiled a little. "And not precisely because I think Jane is such a good judge of character. She tends to approve of people solely on the basis of their horsemanship, which is not always the best test of true worth."

Laura smiled in response. "I know. She disapproved of me fiercely because I wore a new riding habit and she thought I was a *poseur*." Anne laughed, and Laura continued, "What has convinced you, then, Lady Rayleigh?"

"Jane says David likes Lord Dartmouth tremendously," Anne replied promptly. "Unlike his wife, *he* is an excellent judge of character."

Jane nodded complacently. "It's true. David's judgment is infallible."

Anne smiled with affectionate amusement at her husband's niece. "Of course, the final proof of Lord Dartmouth's sterling character came when Jane told me she liked Lord Dartmouth too, even though he was hopeless on a horse."

"He is not hopeless," Laura said indignantly. "And I'd like to see you try to sail a ship, Jane!"

"On a horse Mark is adequate," Jane said flatly. "It's true. *You* know that."

"I understand you yourself are more up to Jane's standard," Lady Rayleigh murmured.

"Laura rides splendidly," Jane said with enthusiasm. "Mark might make a decent rider if he were interested, but he isn't."

"Not interested in horses, and yet Jane likes him." Lady Rayleigh's tone was incredulous. "He must be a marvel," she said to Laura.

"He is." Laura, to her own horror, sounded a little tearful. "He is a wonderful man, and some vicious person is trying to destroy him."

"Well," said Anne practically, "we shall just have to find out who it is. Jane says you think it might go back to Caroline."

"Yes."

Anne nodded. "I remember her. She was the Incomparable of her Season. Now, here is what we shall do." She looked at the two younger women to make certain she had their attention; they were both staring at her with satisfactory intentness. "I am holding a ball in three days' time to which you will all come. In the meanwhile, I shall prepare a list of the men who were dangling after Caroline Gregory six years ago. I'll invite as many of them as are still in town, and we'll all make a point of speaking to them. Then we'll compare our impressions and see if we've reached any conclusion." Laura and Jane both thought Lady Rayleigh's idea was excellent and engaged to appear at Rayleigh House in three days' time, spouses in tow.

The three days before the ball were very busy. Jane and Laura went shopping. Both of them needed court gowns for the coronation, and both needed to augment their wardrobes to meet the demands of London. Mark went to the Admiralty and met with friends from the Royal Society. He came home from these encounters feeling more confident about his reception in London than he had dreamed possible. The rumors had reached the naval and the scientific communities, but the men of his world made it plain that they were sticking by him. He had felt, he confided to Laura, like hugging them.

His one assay into the fashionable world went better than he expected also. He went to Brooks's with David, and though there was a bit of restraint and a great deal of unobtrusive curiosity, everyone he met was polite. "It was because of David," Mark told Laura. "One could see them all thinking: Well, if *Wymondham* is sponsoring the fellow, he can't be all that bad."

Laura laughed. "Is David considered such a font of wisdom?"

"I think it's more that everyone likes him so much. He got quite friendly with a number of fellows during the trial, he told me. Fellow sufferers and all that. The few chaps he introduced me to today were damn nice, in fact."

"It's strange to think that we've only known the Wymondhams for a few months," Laura said musingly. "It seems as if we've been friends for ages. And Jane in particular doesn't seem to make friends very quickly, yet she has been so tremendously good to me. Even Lady Rayleigh seemed surprised by her."

Mark smiled at her tenderly. "I understand it perfectly," he said. "In some ways, you know, you're very like David. Which is probably why *I* like him so much."

Laura looked startled. "Do you think so?"

"Yes," he said, "I do. And now tell me—have you seen Dr. Danbury yet?"

Laura had never felt better in her life. "Do you know," she said a little hesitantly, "I thought I would wait. I'm feeling much better."

"Yes, I thought you seemed to be," he agreed blandly. "However, I want you to see him anyway. After all, it's why you came to London."

She met his brown eyes and knew he was going to hold her to it. He knew she had used Danbury as an excuse, but he was going to call her bluff.

"All right," she sighed in resignation. "I'll make an appointment."

"Good," he replied, grinned at the expression on her face, and left the room saying, "That'll teach you to tell tales to *me*."

Two weeks before the coronation, the Marquis and Marchioness of Rayleigh held a great ball and the whole world came to it. Laura had spent more time on her appearance than she had ever done in her life. She wore a gossamer gown of pale lemon silk over a creamy satin slip. The dress was deeply decolleté, and around her neck she wore the Dartmouth diamonds. Her hair was dressed simply, á la Grecque, and on the shining brown crown of her head she wore the Dartmouth diamond tiara. Pregnancy agreed with her. Her skin bloomed, her breasts swelled full and firm in their yellow silk, her waist was still slender and supple.

Mark's eyes widened when he saw her. "You look good enough to eat," he said. "What a waste to spend the evening at a ball."

She smiled serenely up at him. "We are going out to do battle." She regarded his tall figure with approval. "You look splendid, darling." She handed him her cloak. "Jane and David are waiting downstairs. Avanti."

Anne had done her homework well and had collected four men who at one time had been serious suitors of Caroline Gregory. The Marquis thought she was mad. "Good God, Anne," he said when she confided in him. "Worthington! Dullest chap I ever met. And the others are all of the first respectability. You've got bats in your belfry, my girl, if you think any of them are going about trying to kill Lady Dartmouth."

"You would have said the same thing about Julian Wrexham, Edward," Anne replied firmly.

As this comment was indisputably true, Lord Rayleigh ceased to argue. But his skepticism remained, and as the ball progressed, his wife had to confess she found herself sharing it. Caroline's ex-suitors, those four at least who had remained unmarried, were all depressingly worthy. Jane and Laura came to the same lowering conviction. "There isn't even a *hint* of thwarted passion among the lot of them," Laura mournfully confided to Jane. They had both retired to a bedroom, ostensibly to fix their hair.

"There isn't a hint of passion, period," replied Jane, equally gloomy. "David says he never met such a set of dull dogs in his life. I'm afraid we've wasted an evening."

"It hasn't been wasted," Laura replied. "Before we came to town, everyone was convinced Mark was a murderer; now they are not so sure." She smiled at her friend. "It's all *your* doing, Jane, yours and David's."

Jane looked back at Laura and answered soberly, "It is mainly your doing, Laura. No one who sees you and Mark together could possibly ever believe he was trying to kill you."

And Jane was right. More than her friendship, more than the gracious sponsorship of the Rayleighs, more than the championship of the Admiralty Lords, it was the expression on his wife's face when she looked at him that told the world Mark was innocent.

"Well, it's obvious Lady Dartmouth don't believe her husband's trying to make away with her," Lady Jersey said to Lady Morton as both countesses watched Laura and Mark together on the dance floor. They were waltzing, and Mark's head was bent to listen to something his wife was saying. A look of faint amusement came over his face as he replied. The music stopped but they remained linked together for another moment, light and dark brown heads tilted toward each other, absorbed in themselves. Then Laura glanced around and laughingly stepped back from her husband. He slipped a guiding hand under his wife's arm and they walked together off the floor, both their faces suddenly a little grave. There was about them a sense of natural and inevitable togetherness which was oddly impressive. "I don't believe it's true at all," Lady Jersey said suddenly.

"I believe I must agree with you, Sally," replied Lady Morton. "But whatever is going on that such rumors should arise?"

23

Laura was feeling very discouraged the day after the Rayleigh ball and she and Jane drove into town to visit Lady Maria, who was in residence at Cheney House in Berkeley Square. Lady Maria had been terribly upset by all the rumors, and the three ladies had a long and fruitless conversation trying to fathom out the villain. In consequence, Laura felt even more discouraged as they drove home.

They arrived at Hawkhurst House to find Giles Gregory on the point of departing. He had been in town since May, he told Laura as they returned into the house and sat in the gallery. He had not been at the Rayleigh ball last evening; he and the Marquis traveled in different circles.

They conversed generally for a short while and then Jane said with her usual directness, "Have you heard these rumors about Lord Dartmouth, Sir Giles?"

Giles looked startled, as well he may. It was

a subject Laura had always refused to discuss. "Yes," he said, "I have."

"Well, we're trying to get to the bottom of them," Jane went on briskly. "Perhaps you could help us."

Giles looked at Laura. "You were attacked, Laura," he said gently. "Have you told Lady Wymondham the whole?"

"Yes, I have." Laura returned his look steadily. "Someone damaged the wheel of my phaeton; someone tampered with my boat; someone shone a mirror into the eyes of my mare. But that someone was not Mark. We are trying to find out who it was."

"I know you are fond of him, Laura," he said even more gently than before, "and there is no doubt he is a brilliant young man. But I have been worried about you . . ."

"No need to worry, Sir Giles," said Jane. "*I* am looking out for Laura. I am very happy to see you. I wish to ask you a few questions about your sister."

Giles went very white. "Jane!" Laura protested.

"I'm sorry if it distresses you to talk about her," Jane went relentlessly on, "but under the circumstances it is necessary. You see, we think these attacks against Mark stem from the death of your sister."

Giles turned pain-filled blue eyes on Jane. "Attacks against Mark?" he said faintly. "It is Laura who has been attacked, Lady Wymondham."

"No." Jane was decisive. "Laura was only a way to get to Mark."

"But why?" Giles almost whispered.

198

"That is what we don't know. Now, Sir Giles, tell us: did your sister have anyone who might have cause to hate Mark for marrying her?"

"Not any more than other girls who choose one suitor over another. Caroline *chose* Mark, you see. He was not a husband she had forced upon her."

Giles was looking distinctly shadowy about the eyes and mouth, and Laura intervened. "That is enough, Jane. I'm certain if Giles could help us he would." She firmly changed the conversation, and in five more minutes Giles took his leave.

Their investigations seemed to be getting them nowhere, yet Laura remained convinced that the answer lay with Caroline. That night she and Mark went over it all again. "If there's any clue, it must lie at Castle Dartmouth," Laura said finally. "She didn't go anywhere else after your marriage. But I've lived there for over four years now; if she had left a diary or something, I would have come across it."

"Actually, she did leave Castle Dartmouth once," Mark said slowly. "Just before her death, in fact. She went up to London for a week to do some shopping."

"Mark! She must have met the saboteur while she was in London."

"Perhaps." He rubbed his eyes. "God, Laura, this whole story sounds like something out of Mrs. Radcliffe. It's unbelievable."

"Nevertheless, it is happening. Tomorrow I'm going down to Cheney House and take the place apart. We were there only two weeks after our marriage. I didn't even use all the drawers in the bedroom."

True to her word, Laura descended upon Berkeley Square the following morning. Lady Maria had a breakfast engagement but she told Laura to go ahead and search wherever she chose. Laura was alone. Matthew had developed a fever and Jane did not like to leave him, so David had dropped her off before he went up to Tattersall's. He was to call for her on his way home.

She found it in the first half-hour of her search. It was in the desk in the Countess' bedroom, pushed all the way to the back behind stacks of engraved writing paper. Slowly Laura drew out the small leather-tooled book, and when she opened it and saw the handwriting, her heart gave one hard jolt and then began to race. Mark's name leaped out at her almost immediately. Slowly she took the diary to the window seat and began to read.

The entries started in January of 1815, several months after her marriage. Laura's initial excitement began to give way to deep depression as she read. Caroline meticulously recorded all the minutiae of her days, but made no mention of what was going on in her mind or heart.

It was the entry of September 4 that riveted Laura's attention. The neat, precise handwriting had degenerated into a scrawl. On a page by itself Caroline had written: "He has come back and it has started all over again. Oh, God, what am I to do?"

Laura went very pale as she stared at those words, and then slowly she turned the page. The next entry was dated London, September 18. It read: "There is nothing to be done. For me, nothing. I have before me no escape, no hope, no prospect of peace. I love him. God help me."

That was all. Except that Caroline had gone back to Castle Dartmouth and on October 2 she had killed herself. Tears were running down Laura's face and she sat for quite some time by the sunny window, her face bent over the tragic little book.

Then she rose, wrote a note, went downstairs, and told the butler to summon a hackney for her. "Have this note delivered to Lord Dartmouth at the Admiralty," she instructed the butler coolly, "and tell Lord Wymondham when he calls that I have gone back to Hawkhurst House in a hackney."

"Very good, my lady," said the bulter impassively. In five minutes she was in the cab and on her way home.

Laura was in her bedroom waiting for him when Mark arrived back at Hawkhurst House half an hour after she had. "Did you find something?" he asked almost before the door had fully closed behind him.

"Yes," she said, "a diary. She must have pushed it into the back of the desk drawer and then forgotten it. She was . . . upset."

Laura's voice sounded thin and strange even to her own ears. "Did she say who?" Mark asked sharply.

She shook her head. "No. But perhaps you might guess." She handed him the small leather-bound book. "The last two entries," she said. "All the rest is useless."

Mark opened the book and read. "God," he said. "The poor girl." He was very pale. He gave Laura back the book as if he couldn't bear to hold it.

"Evidently she did not see her lover at all after her marriage until September 4, when he came back. Evidently they also resumed their affair." Laura was forcing herself to speak calmly and logically. "That is why she killed herself, Mark, because she was still in love with this unknown man."

"But if she loved this other fellow, why the devil did she marry me?" he cried in frustration.

"Obviously because she couldn't marry *him*," she answered. "Probably he was married already." She leaned a little toward him. "Think, darling. Did anything happen in the beginning of September that year? Did any new people come into the neighborhood?"

"Let me look at that diary again," he said, and held out a hand. Laura gave him the book. "Let me try to remember," he muttered as he flipped through the pages. "All right. On September 3 the Countisburys had a big party. I remember that. They had a house party of people from London, and Mr. Hamilton was among them. I remember we talked about trying to get around Croker. He is the First Secretary of the Admiralty and has little use for hydrography. I was certain that when I was offered the Turkish survey it was largely due to

202

Hamilton's influence, and so I remember that party very well."

"Yes. Caroline notes the party as well. But she doesn't seem to have met her lover at that time. The note that says he has come back refers to the day after the party." She pointed to the relevant entry. "See."

"No," said Mark. Laura looked up at him. All the blood had drained from his face. "No," he said again, but this time in almost a whisper. "It can't be."

"What can't be, darling?" She stared at him in fear, at his dreadful white face, his dark, horror-filled eyes.

"The day after the Countisbury party," Mark said hoarsely, "Giles came home."

There was a moment of silence. "No!" Laura had her hands straight out in front of her, as though she would physically push the dreadful words away. "No, Mark, it can't be!"

There was sweat on his forehead. "He went over to the Continent soon after we were married," he went on steadily, his voice in direct contrast to his shaking hands. "He came back the following summer, soon after Waterloo, but he stayed in London. I remember thinking it odd he had not come home in time for Robin's christening. He arrived in Dartmouth the day after Lady Countisbury's party. I remember Caroline teasing him about having missed it."

Silence fell and they stared at each other with horror-filled eyes. "If it's true, it accounts for a great deal," Laura finally whispered. Her lips felt stiff.

"Yes, it does." He looked very dark under

the eyes. "It accounts for the kind of despair that would drive her to kill herself."

"Yes." Laura's eyes were almost black. "What she must have felt."

"What Giles must have felt," he said somberly.

Laura's breath sucked in with an audible gasp as full realization hit her. "It was Giles," she said. "Giles who has been arranging the accidents, spreading the rumors."

Mark was staring blindly at the carpet and seemed not to hear her. "It makes sense," he said at last, answering her. "He had the opportunity. He knew your habits."

"But, Mark," she said in great bewilderment, "he wanted to marry me, once. How could he want to hurt me so much?"

He looked up, his attention arrested. "I didn't know that," he said.

"Oh, it wasn't a grand passion, I don't mean that. When I saw where he was heading, I let him know I wasn't interested."

"And then you married me."

"Why, yes, but . . ." Her voice trailed off and she stared at him.

"How Giles must hate me," he said dully.

"When I think of it," Laura said very slowly, "he has always downgraded you. He did it so gently, so mournfully, that one hardly noticed what damning things he implied. He always insisted that you were a brilliant young man. His theory was that being sent to sea so early had hardened your character."

Mark rubbed his forehead as if it were aching. "I wish it had," he said. "Christ, Laura, what a damnable situation."

"I know. We can't expose him. There's Robin." She went, if possible, even whiter. "My God, Robin. That means that Giles may be . . ."

"It alters nothing about Robin," he said strongly. "He is who he is. But you're right, no one must ever find this out." They sat in silence for perhaps five minutes, each absorbed in his own thoughts. Then Mark said, "I may have an idea. I have to think about it for a bit."

"Can I help?" she ventured.

He didn't smile, but his features seemed to soften. "You already have," he said. "You always do."

"What about Jane and David? They know I went to Cheney House to search for a clue. What shall we tell them?"

He stood quietly for a minute, thinking. "Don't tell them anything yet. I'm going into London to call on my solicitor. When I get back, I may have a way to handle this situation."

"All right," she replied, and watched with troubled eyes as he walked out of the room. She shut her eyes and wished desperately that Robin was there so she could hug him.

24

The afternoon dragged interminably for Laura. She gave out that she had a headache and hid in her bedroom. She was afraid to see Jane, afraid to see anyone. Her initial horror had given way to a feeling of sick dread. What was going to happen to them all?

It was almost six o'clock when Mark finally returned. Laura saw him on the drive from her bedroom window, talking to David. The two of them turned and walked up to the house together, still deep in conversation. They disappeared into the side door of the house, and Laura began to pace her room. The few minutes before Mark appeared seemed like an age, but when finally he arrived at her door, she forced herself to take a chair and sit quietly waiting for him to speak.

"I talked to Murray and I think I know how we can handle Giles," he said, taking a chair across from her. His shoulders were slumped with weariness, his face was still and old beyond its years. "I shall have to have it out with him, of course."

Laura's hands clasped together so tightly that the knuckles showed white, but her voice was quiet and calm. "He's dangerous," she said.

"I know. David will come with me—as a bodyguard."

"Have you told him?"

"Only some of it. I told him that Giles was the saboteur, that he hated me because he blamed me for Caroline's death and because he blamed me for marrying you."

She thought for a moment, her brow puckered. "But, Mark, if he is supposed to have loved me so much, why would he try to hurt me?"

"Because, Laura, he is not completely sane." His mouth twisted. "God knows, that at least is true. His mind is certainly a little unhinged to have caused him to want revenge as he did."

"He must have been tormented by guilt," she replied somberly, "and to escape from blaming himself, he blamed you."

"Caroline must have been trying to escape as well; that must be why she married me. And I failed her." His head was bent and Laura slipped out of her chair to go and kneel in front of him.

"This tragedy was not of your making, darling," she said.

He looked down into her upturned face and held her hands tightly. "I didn't help."

"I doubt if anyone could have. It was her own guilt and horror that destroyed her. It wasn't you she couldn't live with, it was herself."

He drew her against him and held her tightly,

his eyes closed. "My little love," he said at last, shakily. "Always so calm and sweet and *sane.*" After a while she felt his hold on her relaxing, and she sat back a little on her heels.

"What are you going to tell Giles?" she asked.

"I'm going to tell him we found Caroline's diary. I'm going to tell him it reveals their incestuous relationship. I'm going to tell him I have lodged it with my solicitor, to be opened in the event of either of our deaths under suspicious circumstances."

Laura's eyes were wide and dark in her pale face. "Have you done that?"

"No. I destroyed the diary."

"But what did you see Mr. Murray about?"

"I am also going to promise Giles that I will keep quiet about his culpability in your accidents if he promises to leave the country. If he comes back, I will publish a copy of his confession to the world. It's the confession that will be lodged with Mr. Murray."

"Will he make a confession?"

"I hope so. At any rate, I'm going in to see him now. David will come with me and wait outside—just to make certain I come back out."

She looked up at him steadily, his beloved face blurred by the tears she was holding back. He looked so tired. "I suppose you must go," she said in a low voice.

He looked back at her, and his mouth curved in a faint yet very tender smile. "No fuss," he said. "No admonitions to be careful. Only 'I suppose you must go.' There isn't another woman like you in the world, Laura."

She managed to smile back at him, and only

after he had left to go face his hate-filled enemy did she break down and cry.

At seven o'clock she went downstairs to join Jane for dinner. They ate in unaccustomed silence, inhibited by the presence of the servants from talking about what was on their minds. When the final course was served, Jane dismissed her attendants and she and Laura settled down for a talk. David had told his wife the identity of the saboteur.

"I didn't like that fellow at all," Jane said flatly. "Now I know why."

"I always thought I liked him," Laura returned, her clear brow furrowed a little in puzzlement.

"Well, you didn't like him enough to want to marry him."

"That's true, but I always assumed that was because he reminded me . . ." She broke off and flushed as she realized what she had almost said.

"Whom did he remind you of?" Jane asked curiously.

"My first husband," said Laura woodenly.

Jane looked unimpressed. "Oh. Well, if your first husband was like Giles, I don't imagine you liked him very much either."

"No," sighed Laura. "I'm afraid I didn't."

Jane leaned forward and lowered her voice. "If I were you, Laura, I should want Giles dead."

Laura stared at her. "Dead?" she echoed blankly.

"Certainly. This business of making him leave

the country is all very well, but you'll be safer if he's out of your way permanently."

"I see." Laura was gazing at her in fascination. "What do you suggest, Jane?"

"I don't suppose you could get rid of him yourself," Jane said with regret. "It would be too complicated. You'll just have to hire someone to do it for you."

"Hire someone to kill Giles for me," Laura repeated.

"Yes," agreed Jane. She was deadly serious. "And it's no use telling Mark *he* ought to do it. Men are so squeamish about things like that."

"I know." There was a suspicious tremor in Laura's voice, but Jane seemed not to notice. "It would be just like them to boggle at a little thing like murder."

"David was actually *sorry* when Julian fell off that cliff," Jane said in exasperated indignation.

"Jane, if you were in my place, would you really hire someone to kill Giles?"

"No. If I thought someone was trying to hurt David, I would kill him myself." Jane's eyes were blazing and Laura looked at her in awe. "You are more civilized than I, however," Jane continued, "so I recommend you hire someone."

As she concluded this piece of advice, the door opened and David came into the dining room alone. "Where's Mark?" Laura asked, going very white.

"He's in the library," David reassured her hastily. "He's fine, Laura, there's nothing to worry about. He got Gregory's confession, but I rather think he'd like to tell you about it himself."

Laura rose instantly. "I'll go to him." David went to sit by his wife as Laura walked swiftly out of the room.

Mark was standing leaning against the chimneypiece when Laura quietly entered the library. He didn't see her at first; he was too busy staring with abstracted concentration at the pattern of the oriental rug.

"Mark?" she said softly. He looked up, pushed himself off from the chimneypiece, and without a word walked straight into her arms.

It took some time for the whole story to finally emerge. It had been a shattering interview. "Giles just sort of collapsed when I told him about the diary," Mark said. "It was terrible to watch. He ... shriveled up before my eyes. I could have borne it better if he'd defied me. But he never tried to deny it. I think perhaps he was even glad to be found out, glad to be forced to stop."

"He agreed to go abroad?" she asked.

"Yes. He agreed to everything I suggested. I have never seen a man so utterly defeated."

"He signed a confession admitting to arranging my accidents?"

"Yes. He sabotaged the phaeton and the boat. He was going to find an excuse not to go out with you that day, you know. He just wanted to make sure *you* got in the boat."

"And the mirror?"

"Yes. He was hiding in the trees. He knew you would come back over the ha-ha." Mark rumpled his hair in the way he always did when he was tired. "It seems he got the idea of making it look as if I were trying to kill you after the incident at Dartmouth Castle. That, apparently, *was* an accident."

They were sitting side by side on the sofa, and now Laura put her cheek against his shoulder and closed her eyes. "The nightmare is almost over, then."

"It *is* over," he replied firmly. "Giles is leaving for France tomorrow."

"Leaving you still surrounded by all those horrid suspicions."

"The talk will die down when no more accidents occur," he said tranquilly. "It won't be so bad."

They sat together peacefully for a few minutes, and then Laura said mischievously, "Jane told me to hire someone to kill Giles."

"What!" Mark pulled away from her and stared down into her amused face. "Did she really?"

"Yes. But she advised me not to tell you. Men, she said, are so squeamish about things like that."

Mark began to laugh. "Only Jane," he said. "I'll wager she was perfectly serious, too."

"She was. She made me feel as if I were a poor-spirited little dab of a thing."

He hugged her to his side. "Not poor-spirited," he said, "but certainly too tenderhearted to ever dream of hurting anyone, even your worst enemy." He stopped laughing and looked down into her lovely, smoky eyes. "I'll wager even further that you're sorry for Giles."

A faint, rueful smile touched her mouth. "I am," she admitted.

"Yes," he said with infinite sadness. "The damnable thing is, so am I."

25

Giles left for France the following day, as he had promised; both Mark and David saw him onto the boat. A few days after his departure, Laura and Mark removed from Hawkhurst to Cheney House in town. It was time, Mark said, that they began to lead a normal life.

It was a course of action more easily prescribed than carried out. It seemed to Laura, as she wondered why she could not relax and enjoy the whirl of social events they were caught up in, that she had never really lived a normal life. She had never had a chance just to be young. Always her life had been shadowed: by her unhappy first marriage, her fear of losing Robin, her fear that Mark did not love her, her fear that he was trying to kill her, her fear that something would happen to him. . . . In retrospect, it seemed she had spent all the years of her young womanhood under some shadow or other. It was not so easy just to step out into the sunlight and forget.

Sometimes she felt as if she were a thousand years old.

The culmination of their London sojourn came on July 19, 1821, when George IV was formally crowned King of England. Mark, magnificently attired in his state robes, and Laura, gorgeous in full court dress, joined the procession of peers and peeresses that gathered in Westminster Hall at ten A.M. Laura, looking around curiously, spotted Jane and David and waved. In a moment the Wymondhams had joined them. Jane and Laura were commiserating with each other about the ostrich feathers they were both obliged to wear in their hair, when Mark nudged his wife. It was the King.

He was splendidly dressed in a twenty-seven-foot-long train of crimson velvet emblazoned with gold stars, and a black Spanish hat that had great plumes of ostrich feathers. He wore a wig whose curls fell gracefully over his forehead.

"Well, at least *one* man is wearing ostrich feathers," Laura whispered to Mark before sinking down in a deep curtsy.

The procession formed up and at last slowly started moving from the Hall to Westminster Abbey. It was headed by the King's Herb-Woman and six maids, who scattered herbs along the way. They were followed by the chief officers of state bearing the crown, the orb, the scepter, the sword of state; and with them were three bishops carrying the paten, chalice, and Bible. The peers, in the order of their rank, moved majestically after the bishops. The King walked under a canopy of cloth-of-gold borne by Barons of the Cinque Ports. As he entered Westminster Abbey, he was greeted by the "Hallelujah Chorus."

It was a very long ceremony. Too long, Laura thought as she moved her head restlessly. All of her ostrich feathers felt as if they were sticking straight into her head. One of the high points was the sermon in which the King was reminded that the most essential service that a sovereign can render to state is to encourage morality and religion. At these words Jane, who had never forgiven the King for making David attend the trial of the Queen for adultery, snorted. Quite audibly. There were smothered smiles all around them, and Mark's shoulders shook suspiciously. After that it all became unbearably long and dull.

Finally it was over and they were allowed to leave the Abbey and go back to Westminster Hall for the banquet. The Hall had been completely transformed for the occasion. A wooden floor had been laid on top of the original stone; the walls had been draped; there were tiers of wooden galleries for spectators, and a dining table for peers and bishops ran the length of the Hall. The King and the Royal Dukes sat at the south end of the Hall at a platform draped in scarlet and gold. At the north end there was a triumphal Gothic arch, and above this arch was a gallery for the orchestra.

There was only one thing wrong with the arrangements, thought Laura to herself as she ruefully surveyed the splendor below her. The three hundred and twelve people sitting down to dinner with the King and his brothers were all male. She, along with the rest of the peeresses, was sitting up in the gallery as a spectator. She had a sudden strange feeling, as she gazed down at the scene below her, that this was exactly what she had been ever since they first came to London: a spectator, incapable of joining in with the fun and gaiety of all the others at the party.

Down below, there was a procession of attendants coming through the Gothic arch bearing the first course. The smell wafted up to Laura, and her nostrils twitched. "I'll be damned if I ever let Prinny have another one of my paintings," Jane muttered darkly at her shoulder. "This is really the outside of enough!"

At the peers' table David murmured something to Mark, who was sitting next to him. Mark nodded and then looked up at Laura in the gallery. She knew instinctively that he was feeling exactly as she was. She smiled at him, and the lines of reserve eased from his face. He smiled back.

Suddenly there was a trumpet roll, and through the Gothic arch came three of his Majesty's chief peers: the Lord High Constable, who was the Duke of Wellington; the Lord High Steward, who was the Marquis of Rayleigh; and the Deputy Earl Marshal, who was Lord Howard of Effingham. These gentlemen all were correctly attired in their state robes. They were also on horseback.

Laura stared in awe-stricken surprise. Down on the floor, Mark turned to David. "I don't believe it," he said in stifled tones.

David was frowning. "Only an idiot like Prinny would dream of bringing horses into a banquet," he said, his eyes on the Marquis' gray.

Up in the gallery Jane was leaning dangerously over the rail, watching her uncle. Laura grabbed her dress and hauled unceremoniously. Suddenly Jane giggled. "You should see Uncle Edward's face. Alcibiades isn't going to stand for this, and he knows it."

"Here comes the meat," said Laura. Her voice was shaking.

Halfway through the meat course, the Marquis' horse decided he had had enough. The Marquis, who had done his part in the ceremony under loud protest, completely lost his temper and began to curse audibly.

Down at the peers' table, Mark buried his face in his hands. "I feel like I'm dining in a circus," he said to David when he got his breath back.

"Poor Uncle Edward," said Jane.

Laura, her eyes brimming, answered after a minute, "Poor Alcibiades."

The three horsemen withdrew, but peace did not reign for long. There was a new fanfare, and through the Gothic arch came a horseman on a white charger, in full armor, with a plumed helmet and carrying a gauntlet.

Mark finished his glass of wine and started on another. "Not a circus," he said. "A tournament."

The tournament did not materialize, however. The King's Champion threw his gauntlet down three times but, prudently, no one accepted his challenge. The King then rose and drank to his Champion out of a gold cup; next he drank to his peers. His peers responded by drinking to their King and giving him several rounds of hearty cheers.

"M-Mark is getting drunk," said Laura.

"I wish I were," Jane replied gloomily.

Finally, after a great deal of further ceremony, the King withdrew to Carlton House. Freed of Majesty, horses, gauntlets, and challenges, the peers settled down to enjoy themselves.

"This is outrageous," Jane complained to Laura. "Here we are, I a nursing mother, you a mother-to-be, and we're starving, while those wretches of men . . ." Words failed her.

Down on the floor, Mark and David appeared to be getting progressively merrier. Laura got up and went over to the gallery rail. The din in the Hall from all the voices was deafening. She waved her hand and finally caught Mark's attention. "We're starving," she mouthed at him.

He got up and came over to stand below her. "What?" he bellowed up.

"I said," she shouted back, "that we're . . ."

Silence fell.

". . . starving!" she finished on a shreik that filled the Hall.

Mark stared up at her, and she stared back; the sudden silence echoed around them. They exploded into mirth together.

"J-just a minute," Mark promised, and went over to his place at the table. He was back almost immediately with something wrapped in a napkin. "Catch," he called, and tossed it upward.

Laura leaned out and snared it easily. "Chicken!" she cried, and waved it triumphantly. The Hall broke into laughter and applause.

Laura sat down and gave a piece to Jane. All over the Hall, packages were being tossed from grinning husbands to hungry wives. Laura crunched industriously. She felt very, very happy.

Mark was not drunk when they finally got into their coach to return home, but then, he was not precisely sober, either. He slid down on his spine next to Laura and began owlishly to repeat the challenge of the King's Champion.

"No," Laura said positively, "the best part of the whole day was Lord Rayleigh. Did you *hear* what he said?"

Mark dissolved into laughter. "Oh, God. I did."

"Did you *see* what Alcibiades did?"

"Laura, stop," Mark begged.

Her eyes were full of tears from pent-up laughter. "I can't," she said. "Remember the coronation sermon—"

He interrupted her by shrieking suddenly, "I'm starving, Mark!" and she collapsed against him. It took them a few minutes before they were able to descend from their carriage. Halfway up the stairs, Mark stopped. "Chicken!" he shouted, and waved his arm. That started them all over again.

They staggered into Laura's bedroom together, only to be met by the censorious eye of her new dresser. Mason was very dignified, very proper, and had absolutely no sense of humor. The only reason Laura had kept her was that she was a genius with hair. Under her forbidding pale gaze, Laura struggled to sober up. "Your ostrich feathers were a huge success, Mason," she offered.

"Indeed, my lady." The gimlet eye regarded Laura's feathers. They had become somewhat disarranged in the coach.

Mark backed up, collapsed into a chair, and stretched his long legs out in front of him. Mason looked outraged. "The best ostrich feathers in the whole damn place," he said solemnly.

"They were, Mason, truly," Laura said hastily, and gave Mark a quelling look. Her husband, however, was completely out of control.

"Everyone said so," he went on relentlessly. "Even the King. 'Dartmouth,' he said to me, 'who did your wife's ostrich feathers? Best damn ostrich feathers I have ever seen. Dashed if I'm not going to appoint the woman who did those ostrich feathers to my own household!' "

Mason stared at her mistress's husband as he lounged at his ease in his wife's bedroom, where, she considered, he had no right to be. At least until his wife was undressed and properly in bed. "My lord . . ." she began with great dignity.

Mark looked at the ceiling and began to sing. It was something to do with the reproduction of the ostrich. It was regrettably bawdy and excruciatingly funny.

"Mason," Laura gasped, feeling as if she would explode any moment, "go to bed. Please."

"Are you quite certain you don't require my assistance, my lady?"

"I . . . Quite certain, thank you. Good night."

The door had scarcely closed behind her before Laura fell on the bed sobbing. "Oh, God," she wailed, holding her side, "I think I'm going to die! Stop!"

Mark stopped in mid-note and moved on silent feet to the bed. Laura did not hear him and was surprised to feel his hand on her shoulder. He turned her over on her back and she looked up into the lean masculine face that was now so close to hers. "The feathers have got to go," he said, and began to remove them from her coiffure. In the process, her long dark hair somehow became unpinned and fell loosely onto the satin bedspread. Mark put two hands on either side of her head. His face was quite close to hers.

"I didn't think I could laugh like that," Laura said weakly.

"You and I are going to take a proper honeymoon," said Mark. His face was now very close.

"We are?"

"Yes. Without Robin. Just you and me. And you'll learn how to laugh again, I promise you." His voice was very deep and very tender.

She put a hand up and ran her fingers through his sun-bleached hair. "I've been feeling so . . . distant lately," she said.

"I know." He kissed her ear, her chin, her mouth, her ear again. "But it's all finished with, sweetheart. It's safe to be happy." Her hand moved from his hair to his cheek. He understood, she thought; he understood how difficult it had been for her. "I love you, Laura," he said.

She smiled up at him. "Are you sure it isn't my ostrich feathers?"

He growled. "Much as I love your ostrich feathers, I love you even better without them. In fact, I love you best without anything at all."

"Lord Dartmouth!" she protested, scandalized.

"And since you so inconsiderately sent your dresser away, I suppose I'll have to do the job myself."

Laura fixed her eyes on the ceiling. "All hail the noble ostrich," she began to sing. "Oomph!" This was as Mark's full weight descended upon her. He wrapped his arms around her and rolled so that they were both on their sides, facing each other. Laura smiled. "This dress will never be the same."

"No matter," he replied softly. "I'll buy you another."

"Mark . . ." She was looking straight into his golden-brown eyes. Her breath caught a little in her throat. "I love you so much," she said.

"Do you?" he slid a caressing hand over her hip. "Show me how much."

"Mmn," she replied. And did.

AUTHOR'S NOTE

Mark's career is based on the early career of Francis Beaufort, the famous English hydrographer, whose survey of the south Turkish coast in the frigate *Fredericksteen* served as model for the fictional expedition I assigned to Mark.

ABOUT THE AUTHOR

Joan Wolf is a native of New York City who presently resides in Milford, Connecticut, with her husband and two young children. She taught high school English in New York for nine years and took up writing when she retired to rear a family. Her previous books—THE COUNTERFEIT MARRIAGE, A KIND OF HONOR, A LONDON SEASON, A DIFFICULT TRUCE, THE SCOTTISH LORD, HIS LORDSHIP'S MISTRESS, and THE AMERICAN DUCHESS are also available in Signet editions.